Praise for the

In addition to writing about the ref
and income inequality, Malherbe also
Muslims living in non-Muslim societies. Touches on a variety of
current issues.

- Sarabi, Muslimah Media Watch

The Tower is not so much a place in this story but a person. It
is a living, breathing entity, much like the diverse cast of charac-
ters who reside within. The Tower is a heart-warming novel that
answers the complex question of what it means to call a place
home.

- Nadia, Headscarves and Hardbacks

[Malherbe] seamlessly navigates the plot towards the voices
she wants her readers to hear. Its power lies in incessantly chip-
ping away at statistics, clichés and stereotyping. An important
addition to the arsenal of literary work needed for better under-
standing of and insight into a troubled world that needs to be re-
minded of its values of compassion and empathy, but above all
else, its humanity.

- Rana Asfour, BookFabulous

Shereen Malherbe is a British Palestinian writer whose debut novel, *Jasmine Falling*, features in the Top 20 Best Books by Muslim Women. After studying her B.A. degree in English Literature with Creative Writing, Shereen now combines her two interests of writing and travel to create novels that straddle both the East and West.

Shereen is also a writer and researcher on behalf of Muslimah Media Watch on the representation of Muslim women in the media and pop culture. She has spoken about trending topics including Islamophobia on live TV, resulting in her classification in the Media Diversified Experts Directory.

THE
TOWER

THE TOWER

Shereen Malherbe

First published in the UK by Beacon Books and Media Ltd
Innospace, Chester Street, Manchester M1 5GD, UK.

Copyright © by Shereen Malherbe 2019

www.beaconbooks.net

Cataloging-in-Publication record for this book is available from the British
Library

Paperback ISBN 978-1-912356-22-5
Ebook ISBN 978-1-912356-23-2

Acknowledgements

بسم الله الرحمن الرحيم

Firstly, all praise belongs to God, for giving me the opportunity to be able to write this novel, with my intention being to shine some light on the beauty of Islam and the positive human values that are at the heart of all religious teachings.

Thank you to Beacon Books and Jamil Chishti for allowing me to have this opportunity. A huge thank you to Siema Rafiq, for being a conscientious, kind and thorough editor who has been as dedicated to this book from the first manuscript until the final proofread and everything in between.

Thank you to Cat and Jo for their guidance on my Creative Writing modules. You both provided positive, constructive feedback that helped me in various ways from the creation of ideas, right through to the end of the writing process.

I want to thank my husband for his continued dedication and support; the late nights, the anxieties and all the other difficulties that come with supporting a wife who is an author. To my amazing children, who inspire me with their imagination and creativity that far exceeds my own, you are all the reason that I can explore love and belonging like I have in this novel.

For Sarah, her dedication to reading the first drafts and for her enthusiasm in keeping me going until the end.

For my dad and Ramzieh. Zuzu, you always share your stories so openly and with so much heart that they made the story what it is now. I truly believe that I share what already exists and my inspiration comes from sharing other's stories because I believe they should have a voice.

For my mum, who always believes my writing is the best thing in the world – your belief keeps me going through the long nights and edits!

To my sisters for helping me to write in the early hours of the morning and to Imarniya who gave up her English notebooks so I would have somewhere to write whilst I was traveling. Keep writing your stories and I hope one day, yours become books too.

Lastly but importantly, a big thank you to all my readers. It belongs to you from this point onwards. I want to thank you for allowing this story to be shared with you all.

*Home changes. When you leave and go back,
it never feels the same again...*

Chapter 1

~ Leah ~

Leah stood staring up at the great bulk of the tower block. For years in her Kensington Town house she had resented living in its shadow. It greedily sucked up the sunshine on a summer's day, and in the winter, it exacerbated the grey sky. But now that she'd been dropped on its doorstep, it looked even worse. Its wet concrete façade was the colour of a giant slug rising defiantly from the soil. As her eyes glanced up, the windows gathered together like dark eyes, staring down at her. The driver of the removal van had unceremoniously dumped her belongings behind her, but she was too distracted to notice since she was still in shock that this was where she had ended up.

She had never imagined she would have to leave her home behind. She remembered how it had been a gift for her twenty-fifth birthday. That birthday seemed like decades ago, not the short six years it really had been since she had fallen in love with her new home. She had loved its pastel blue frontage the moment she had seen it, with its newly renovated Victorian sash windows almost as tall as her, and the pointed pitch-tiled roof topping it off like a beautiful crown.

Since she had left, she clung on desperately to her pile of belongings and Chesterfield sofa, which now looked ridiculously out of place on the edge of the pavement. She would have liked to have brought her plants but she didn't have a garden. She couldn't even consider bringing the beehive that he had made... before. She would go back, she told herself. This was only temporary.

She sighed heavily and took solace in the fact that Elijah seemed okay, kicking his football against the wall, so she stifled the tears welling at the back of her throat.

Her arrival had drawn a crowd. She looked around hesitantly at the faces appearing in front of her. A few people hung from the windows, smoking. Two men about her age walked towards her. Their white robes came down below the knee, covering wide leg trousers that hung just above their ankles. They walked past her and went straight to the Chesterfield sofa behind her.

'Please don't tell me you're going to try and steal that right in front of me?'

'Are you serious?' the shorter one said, adjusting his white cap. 'You just looked like you needed some help.'

'Oh gosh, I am so sorry. I am not myself today. Sixth floor. I –'

'This is my brother, Mo,' he said, gesturing to his brother, who was still adjusting his cap over his hair. 'He helps even if it ain't wanted.'

Leah couldn't help but see the offence in Mo's face, so she said, 'I am sorry, I-'

'Don't walk off, Nidal,' Mo shouted after him, seemingly more concerned with his brother than with her apology, 'I can't lift it on my own.'

Nidal waved to some lads standing by the main entrance door to the building. 'Give us a hand.'

They came over and between them shifted the over-sized sofa piled full of Leah's belongings into the shady hallway. It didn't amount to much, Leah thought, her cheeks burning. She wanted to say from the exhaustion of it all, but it was more the embarrassment of where she had moved to. Poor Elijah. The last eighteen months had been harder for him. She looked over to where he was playing football. There was no one there.

'Elijah, where are you?' she called, as her eyes flitted around the unfamiliar territory. He wasn't outside. Leah darted inside, frantically pushing the button on the lift, cursing that she had slipped up and let him out of her sight. The lift didn't move. No lights came on. A man dressed in ragged, foul-smelling clothes crawled out of the cleaning cupboard.

Leah let out a squeal.

'Good day, Miss,' he mumbled through broken, brown-stained teeth.

Leah pressed the button harder.

'It don't work, that,' he said, pointing his half-gloved hand towards the lift.

Of course it's broken, she thought, and ran up the stairs looking down each hallway. The hallways lengthened out in front of her. Leah stopped briefly and saw how the sombre corridors spanned from one end of the staircase to the other, broken only by small windows. Slices of dull light cast wells into the hallways, just enough to see the monotonous numbers nailed to each door. Outside of them lay tattered doormats. Chained bicycles blocked the exits.

As she twisted up the fourth staircase, a crowd of kids ran past her. She pressed her body into the wall so they could pass. Reaching the sixth floor, she heard the familiar sound of a plane whizzing through the hallway. The tense feeling started to ease when she saw it was Elijah. He was with Mo, the guy who had taken the sofa upstairs. She couldn't hear what they were talking about.

'Thank you for your help,' she said, marching over and rustling in her pockets, dropping cash and coins on the floor.

'Nah, I don't want money.'

'Oh. Thank you,' Leah said, holding out her hand to shake.

Mo pressed his hand against his chest and headed back towards the stairs. Leah dropped her hand back to her side.

'Wait,' she called, 'do you know there's a strange man hanging around the cleaning cupboard?'

'That's Harold. He cleans around the place sometimes for some extra cash. He's alright.'

'Is it not dangerous to have someone like that in the building?'

'Maybe if he saw your fridge. Otherwise, nah, you ain't got nothing to worry about.'

Leah turned to Elijah. 'Shall we get inside before you make any more new friends?' Leah said, pushing open the door and guiding Elijah inside.

'Later, mate.'

'See you, Mo!' Elijah shouted back.

She closed the door behind her, temporarily relieved to be inside with Elijah next to her, safe. But her relief didn't last long as she glanced around. The walls seemed to close in sharply. The lounge, if you could call it that, was where Mo had put the sofa. It took up most of the room and looked towards a sad, empty TV stand. The open plan kitchen was nothing more than a tiny fridge, an oven and a sink hammered into some faux granite top that made an L-shape cutting into the hallway. Two doors were open just behind the Chesterfield. They were the two bedrooms. A window was on the far, right-side wall.

She walked over, holding Elijah's hand tight enough to squeeze out any disappointment. London spread out below them. Cars weaved through traffic, red buses cut through the city scape of North Kensington, framing a piece of the world that despite living in Kensington her whole life, Leah had never seen before.

Leah took Elijah with her when she went to the shops to stock up on some food staples. It was the first time she had to look at the price of things. She stood there for quite a while debating whether to buy fresh milk or settle for the powdered one which would last them a lot longer. She bought powdered and told Elijah it was only until she had time to clean the fridge.

Back at home, she began to make a pot of rice and added beans. He used to make rice this way, she thought. He would never have let this happen. He was so different to her. After years of being knocked down, he had grown capable and strong. A strength she never had to acquire. The rice stuck to the bottom. It had gone over.

As she dished up the food, she glanced out of the window. One of the steely buildings would be the state school, she thought. A creeping fear rose through her blood as she imagined dropping him off there. No, she couldn't – she had to find a way to pay for his private school. His life must be as close to his normal one as much as possible until she sorted something more permanent back where they used to live. She served dinner and felt some relief in filling her son's stomach with hot food. She couldn't eat a thing but couldn't bear to throw the food away. Since the fridge was switched off, she couldn't keep it. At that moment, in the unusual quietness of the apartment, she glanced around at the brown boxes, the stripped walls echoing the emptiness of the room.

She was used to eating as a family together, the windows flung open, allowing the sounds of the street to drift inside. Sounds of bicycles, their wheels spinning on the pavement and paper bags perched in their baskets catching the wind. Florists delivering fresh mantelpiece arrangements every week: Mondays for the Allerton family and Fridays for the Claytons, in preparation for their evening soirées. Neighbours' kids sitting on the steps in the sunshine, the sound of opening books, pencils on crisp, blank sheets of paper. Blank sheets of promise, an unwritten future, free to make. She looked out of the window and saw that even the sun's rays barely broke through. There was no sound from the street, just odd noises of scraping furniture from the floor above and doors slamming beneath them. There was no colour, no life. None that she knew of. She had to change it for Elijah; he couldn't live like this. She decided she would buy paint, get some colour on the walls. A family table. Then the realisation smacked across her heart. There would be no family, only the two of them sat together.

'Elijah, please don't put so much food in your mouth at once. It's dangerous. I don't want you to choke.'

'Mummy, I'm not a baby anymore. I'm nearly ten.'

'You're still my baby,' Leah said, ruffling his hair, trying to ignore the sadness of the quiet room.

Once she was satisfied he had finished his lunch, she said, 'Come with me Elijah, I don't like to leave you alone.'

'You used to let me stay at home when you went out.'

'Well, sweetheart, Doris was there then, and I'm sure she will come and work for us again but after... well, you don't need reminding. I don't want you too far from me.'

Elijah grabbed his ball and followed his mum down to the ground floor.

'Go for a kick around if you like. Just stay on the grass so I can see you. I won't be long.'

Leah watched Elijah leave the building's main entrance and turned around in the hallway. At the end of the corridor, the door of the cleaning cupboard was ajar. The smell of bleach and musty air filtered through the crack. She tapped on it gently.

'Excuse me?'

The old man shuffled out, his eyes adjusting to the dim light in the hallway. 'You need help with something?'

'No, no I don't. I just...' Leah thrust the food into his hands and rushed away, looking behind at his bewildered face holding the pot of rice. She walked straight into someone. 'Sorry, I'm sorry,' she said under her breath, keeping her eyes on the floor, worried how a person in a building like this one may react.

'Leah, right?'

Someone knew her name. She looked up and saw Mo.

'What are you doing hanging around the cleaning cupboard?'

She noticed his attention was on Harold. He seemed to smile almost secretly, in a strange way that revealed little. He was at least a foot taller than her with broad shoulders and a strong physique, clear even through the loose T-shirt he wore, yet his eyes looked friendly beneath his strong brows.

Her cheeks flushed. Why did she care that he noticed her charitable deed? She didn't. She excused herself and ran to Elijah on the grass, desperately wanting to look back at the strong figure in the hallway. She turned around, but he had already left.

That night before bed, Leah and Elijah curled up on the mattress on the floor together whilst Leah read his bedtime book. The pictures made her want to cry. The characters were a family who lived in a house with a picturesque garden to play in. But Elijah didn't seem to notice; he had already fallen asleep on her lap. She wanted to stay with him. Keep him close to her. She stayed awake watching the rise and fall of his chest. His heart beat with hers as it did when he was part of her, inside her stomach. She watched the gentle brush of his brown curled eyelashes pressed against his cheeks and knew how tentative it was that he was still breathing. How life could stop in a moment. How a life and the lives entwined within it could be changed forever. Lost. She held onto him so tight she was afraid she would hurt him. She relaxed her grip ever so slightly and lay down next to him, sick with the fear that one day she might lose this part of her and him, and then there would be nothing left.

chapter 2

~ *Reem* ~

'Let me open the door for you,' the social worker said, moving Reem gently out of the way of the door frame she had been looking at vacantly for the last thirty seconds. Reem looked around inside. She barely noticed a thing, except for the window. She went over and stared down into the maze-like city that heaved in a mess of roads and people below her.

'You're one of the lucky ones,' Jane said, walking over to her at the window, 'you've only been here a few months and you already have a home.'

Reem glanced upwards to the sky for some relief, but the curtain of hanging grey sky hid a pale sun. It was not the glowing amber of the sun she knew. The clouds did not hang like gentle wisps in a lucid blue sky. The clouds heaved. Dark. Swollen.

'Please help me find my brother,' Reem pleaded with her social worker, 'he is only ten.'

'I know this is a very difficult time,' Jane replied. 'You must come to the Town Hall to fill out the forms there, so they can begin to search for him.'

Reem looked out of the window at the unfamiliar city. She remembered her old house she had left so many months before. Its wide, open courtyard, the pomegranate trees in the garden. Every year fruit blossomed and was picked from the trees as the mild spring air enveloped the courtyard where she would sit with mama, papa and Adar. He would play in the trees and walk to the mosque barefoot. It was so far removed from the concrete tower in this city. A city she had only ever seen on films or read about in books. The last image of her home morphed away from the courtyard and was replaced by the sound of jet engines slicing through the sky, leaving the neighbour's walls collapsing under the debris and filling the air with choking dust. A child's shoe stuck out, bloody and buried in the branches of the pomegranate tree.

'North Kensington.' Jane paused. 'Did you hear me, Reem?'

Reem's thoughts snapped back to the present.

'I have someone else to visit in the building so I am going to go now, okay?'

Reem didn't answer. The door opened and closed with a loud click as Jane left.

Despite being empty, the apartment began to fill with Adar's voice. It seemed to echo around the walls. She imagined him standing with her. 'It's not so bad, Reem. We can almost see the stadium,' he would say. She would laugh and ask how football could occupy his mind at such a time. She almost smiled until the walls started moving in thick waves. They rolled up and down, crashing into her, until the floor swelled beneath her feet.

She opened the door and ran down the hallway. She had no idea where she was going but she had to leave the confined room, the clinically painted walls, the strip lights hanging like the hospital boat where evil clung to the walls and tried to crawl out. She ran out into the open air. Around her, despite her panic, normality resumed. Couples walked hand in hand. A child flew a kite in the wind. A man with a half-eaten sandwich hanging from his mouth waved to stop a London cab by the side of the road. Everyone continued as though there was no war. No dead children. She grabbed the piece of paper that Jane had given her from her pocket. The address of the Town Hall was written down with some directions of how to get there. Finding it was the first step she had to take so that someone, anyone, could help her to find him.

Reem crossed over the patches of grass and mature trees that broke up the blocks of dreary buildings that surrounded the exit to the tower. She followed the pavement until she reached a road. She knew she had to get on a bus, but which one? One after another followed, the same red colour, two storeys high, hissing and stopping by bus stops with people hopping on and off. The bus signs and routes were drawn in different coloured lines. They crisscrossed over each other, labelled with different numbers. She traced the line that ended up in Kensington town, but she wasn't entirely sure she was planning it correctly.

'Excuse me,' she said to no one in particular after the last bus pulled up and a few people jumped off the steps and onto the street next to her. Her voice was inaudible amongst the screeching of the brakes and the rumble of the engine. The next one came along and the bus driver opened the door for her. She stood there looking at him. He was large around the middle, almost bald and had an accent she hadn't heard before. 'You getting on, love?'

'Town Hall, Kensington.'

'Not this route, wait for the N28.'

She had passed English at school, but here it was too fast, spoken in blurred, hurried accents. She could barely understand the conversations she heard, or the words floating in the air in the busy streets. The doors closed and the bus pulled off. She then wondered about Adar. If he was still alive, how would he cope here?

She began walking, looking in at the shop windows, her nose pressed against the glass as her eyes spied unfamiliar objects. Mismatching used clothes stood lifelessly on hangers. Old misshapen straw hats flopped on top of metal hooks. Yellowing books and shabby game boxes stacked high in the corners. Trays of plastic and metal accessories were labelled in the currency she hadn't worked out yet. Reem wondered what type of shop sold parts of other people's lives. Pulling herself away from the windows, she glanced up at the boxes of houses that clambered up to the skyline, wondering why she had never seen this part of London in the films she had watched as a young girl.

When she finally stopped, she realised she was more lost than ever. She looked up to the skyline but the day was so dim she couldn't tell what time it was. And there, coming behind her in the distance, was the tower. It stared down at her ominously, as though all the time she had tried to leave it, it had hovered in the background, reminding her of the shadow of her life and what it had been reduced to.

She would return home. She would restore the courtyard and the pool for the fruits. The war would finish soon, she consoled herself. But every time she felt her stomach flutter, every time she thought of being without Adar, she wondered if she could ever go back. And if she couldn't return, what was left for her? She thought about it as her footsteps hit the hard concrete paving slabs that looked like gravestones under her feet. Exhausted, she eventually passed the sliver of grass laid out like a mock carpet in front of the building.

Back in the apartment she flung open her tiny suitcase, grabbed her prayer shawl and began to weep and pray. She didn't notice how thin the walls were so when someone knocked at the door, she tensed up. Back home, she would never open the door to someone in case it was a man she didn't know. Her father or her brother had to be in. But since she was alone, she didn't know what to do. Maybe it was Jane? Maybe she had come with news of Adar? She picked up her prayer shawl from around her ankles and ran to the door. She stood with it open for a few seconds, looking at the unexpected visitor on her doorstep. He was a bit taller than Adar, lighter skin. Still a boy, but too well-fed, too clean.

'Hi, I'm Elijah.'

She was too stunned to speak.

'I heard something so I came to check you were okay.'

'I am fine... thank you.' The words that came out of her mouth were slow, carefully pronounced.

'It's just I heard you crying.'

'Oh, I... I'm fine.'

'You sure?'

He looked sweet, confused. Maybe he hadn't understood her accent. She didn't really know what else to say. She stood opposite him for a few moments, glancing back into the apartment. Back home, kids knocked on the doors hoping for sugar and treats. Reem disappeared from the doorway and rustled around in her suitcase. She returned to the door with Elijah still standing there and thrust piles of sweets into his hands.

'You want more?' Reem said, but she was interrupted by a blonde woman – thin like she hadn't eaten in a while but with skin as soft as someone who could afford to wash with rose water every day.

'Don't just go out by yourself Elijah, my goodness, you could be kidnapped.'

'Kidnapped?' Reem repeated, the word feeling alien on her tongue.

'I'm sorry. I'm Leah. My son is not used to living so close to people. We aren't from here.'

'Me neither.'

'South Kensington.'

'Syria.'

Reem waited for words that didn't come. She saw the gap of two worlds stretching in front of them, separating them with a vast distance. She looked down and loosened her gown so it flowed more freely and tried to hide her embarrassment.

Leah fidgeted with Elijah's shirt collar. 'Where did you get these?' she asked him.

Elijah pointed at Reem. She felt as though she had done something wrong.

'What's in them?' Leah said, grabbing one and reading the labels. 'He has allergies.'

Reem smiled although she didn't understand what Leah meant. She spoke as though she was in a hurry. Her words blurred before Reem could work out what she was saying. 'So, if there isn't anything I can help you with, well, we'll be off.'

'Yes, please. I do need some help with something,' Reem said, noticing the woman now hesitating. After a pause, the boy stepped forward as though he was going to come inside. She closed the door just enough so the gap wasn't big enough for him to squeeze through as Reem remembered what else she had unpacked from her suitcase. The thickly wrapped bundle of brown paper and tissue tied with string sat in the middle of the table. If the English woman saw what she had stolen, she wouldn't be able to stay.

'Wednesday?' said Reem.

'Sure, what time?' Leah answered, pulling Elijah away from the door.

'Morning. Thank you,' Reem said, as a sudden impulse took over, encouraging her to shuffle out into the hallway and throw her arms around the startled woman. She took a few steps back into her apartment and closed the door, the weight of guilt beginning to lift slightly. When dawn came the following day she could begin to search for Adar. How hard could it be to find a lost Syrian child on the streets of London? She remembered Adar was on the boat. He had arrived. But with the images in her head, she couldn't be certain of anything.

She curled up on the floor next to the window as dusk fell on the city under a marred moon. She unwrapped one of her parcels and stroked the smooth edges, marvelling at the stained cut glass, impressed with the calligraphy; a remnant of a once beautiful city. A city she belonged to, one she would soon return to. Looking out at the view that made her feel weightless, suspended halfway up to the heavens, she soothed herself to sleep. With her eyes closed, she began to rebuild her old city, restoring her old life piece by piece. When she found Adar, although damaged, she would begin to feel whole.

chapter 3

~ Leah ~

Leah wasn't expecting any visitors so the unusual sound of the doorbell ringing through her apartment startled her. She looked over at Elijah. He was on the computer, his tongue curled to the right as he concentrated, his fingers tapping on the control pad he was yanking back and forth. His cereal bowl was by his leg and the breakfast pots were still on the table. The kitchen was a small U-shape, turning into the lounge, where the bin was overflowing and extra bags were stacked up next to it. She opened the cupboards but there was no space to hide it inside. She hadn't told anyone where she lived. Had her parents found her? She felt sick and embarrassed at the thought. The limited floor space was all she could afford and the landlord only rented it out to her because she gave him all her savings as a deposit. It hadn't looked so bad at the beginning of the week when she moved in. At least then it had been clean. This was just the ammunition her mum needed to confirm how despite being an adult, Leah was incapable of making responsible choices. Flustered, Leah tripped over a bag, the insides of it littering the floor. She pushed it under the breakfast bar, trying to hide it from view, but there was no escaping the oily tuna smell that had leaked all over the floor. She should have thrown the rubbish out the night before, but she wasn't really sure what to do with it. She was on the sixth floor, so it wasn't like at her house where she could just pop outside. She turned on the taps and splashed clean water over the pots. She stood back looking at the mess, thinking that her panicking had actually made it look worse. The bell chimed again.

'Coming,' she said, scooping up clothes from the floor and tossing them into her bedroom, shutting the door behind them. She yanked open the curtains and yelped as they fell off the curtain rail that was nailed into the plaster on the wall. Bits of it crumbled down on top of her hair. She dusted it off and retied her dressing gown, covering her pyjamas.

She opened the door tentatively, peering out to the unfamiliar visitor outside the door. Clipboard, cheap suit, mousy cropped hair and eyes she didn't know, peered through red-framed glasses. It certainly wasn't her mum.

'Ophelia?' the voice said.

'Yes?' Leah shuddered. No one called her that except for her mother.

'I'm glad I caught you. I came a few days ago but you weren't in.'

'I am not buying anything, in fact, we've just moved in and I –'

'I'm not a sales person, Ophelia.'

'No?' Leah was thrown off by the repetition of her name. It made her shudder every time she heard it.

'My name is Jane Taylor. I'm a social worker,' she said, holding up her badge. 'We have received a complaint and I was hoping to come and visit you and Elijah?'

'Who complained? About what?' Leah said, opening the door as Jane insistently stepped forward into the apartment. Leah closed the door quickly, wondering if any of her new

17

neighbours had seen her visitor arrive. She turned to look at the same view from the door. It was packed full of her belongings. She had moved from a decent sized two-bed-room townhouse and had an enviable wardrobe, stacks of belongings, household items, art for the walls, curtains and beddings, and when she had moved she brought as much as she could. It was less than half of what she owned, maybe even a quarter of it, but in this tiny space it filled every corner. Clothes were hanging on makeshift rails and lined the lounge. Boxes of curtains, bedding and linen that she hadn't stored anywhere were still stacked up in the corner. As for the mess and the 18-rated computer game Elijah had been playing, Leah had no excuse.

'You must be Elijah,' Jane said, bending down next to him.

'Yes,' he said, looking towards Leah in confusion. He backed away from Jane and went towards his mum.

'Don't worry, darling. The lady is just here to check we are okay and have settled into our new place.' Leah looked around and then turned to Jane. 'We have only just moved in, you see. I just need to sort some things out.'

Jane didn't answer. She stood up and brushed herself down, beginning to scribble in her notebook. Leah didn't like how Jane sat on the sofa without being invited. How she looked over Elijah as he spoke and how her pen scraped against the paper on her clipboard. Monitoring. Judging.

'Elijah is just fine,' Leah blurted out. She overheard Elijah talking about bones and soil. His preoccupation with the buried had increased and it unnerved Leah that he would come across as so unhinged in front of the social worker. 'We both are. I don't know who reported this non-sense, probably my stuck-up mother who has no reason to except...' Leah paused, her hands shaking slightly as she remembered their last conversation. It replayed clearly in her mind when she had left. 'If you can't look after him, we will take him,' her mother had said. The recollection made Leah give away what was racing around her mind.

'She wants him for herself, she wants to take the last thing I have.'

'I can't tell you who the report was from –'

'It's obvious, who else would it be? Well, you have to go. I am not having my life choices judged just because I can't afford to live where I used to.'

'It really doesn't matter about your location.'

'Well then, what?'

Jane put down her pen and laid her notebook on the sofa. She turned to face Leah. 'Perhaps we should talk about this in private? If that's okay with you, Elijah?'

Elijah frowned. He didn't move from his mum's side.

'Elijah, would you mind playing in your bedroom for a moment whilst I talk to your mum?'

Elijah ignored her request and turned to his mum. His eyes reflected her state of panic. 'Mummy, they won't take me away from you, will they? Is this because I'm not at school? I'm sorry, I will go in. I don't mind, I swear –'

He had been increasingly anxious ever since his father died and this isn't going to help, Leah thought.

'No darling, it isn't anything you've done. It's just a misunderstanding. I will sort it.' Leah tried to keep her voice under control. 'Go and play in your room. We won't be a minute.'

Elijah closed the door softly behind him. Leah's breath quickened when he was out of view. Her arms wouldn't stay still by her side. She chewed the edges of her robe's sleeves. If she wasn't able to look after him, who would? She glanced over at Jane whose back was to her on the sofa. Her official badge hanging around her neck. Leah had heard of these stories where children were taken and then placed into care. Once they were gone, it was difficult to get them back. Some kids became lost in the care system. The thought made her feel sick. She hated herself for not being better. She should have got dressed this morning, she thought. She should have been on top of the housework. It might have turned out differently if she had invited Jane in properly. She could have offered her tea and made her feel welcome. But now she would probably take him just to spite her. Her parents would probably pay her to hand him over. That's what money could do. It could buy people.

'Please, Ophelia, sit down whilst I explain what will happen.'

'You won't take him from me, will you?'

'That's always a last resort. I am here to check on him and to check on you. To see how you're coping.'

Leah looked at her. Clever, she thought. Throw her off guard and then use it against her. 'We are both coping perfectly fine.'

'I understand your husband died eighteen months ago?'

Leah's back straightened up. She hadn't expected this to come up. Rationally, of course, it was a normal question to ask. It was probably the reason her mother gave for Leah's supposed sudden downfall; dropping out of her last few months of medical training, moving out of her house, refusing to live in comfort with her parents. Leah hadn't recognised it was grief and the drive to become her own person away from the claustrophobia of her parents and the pressure they had put on her and Elijah. He was ferried to violin lessons, piano lessons, chess class. He was exhausted. And to her parents, especially her mum, it was everything to become part of the world she inhabited, part of the world Leah and Elijah were slipping away from. Jane spoke but Leah was barely listening. Instead she thought about the state of her life. What her mum had said was true; she was incapable of looking after Elijah by herself. To make it worse, without her parent's money, she could barely afford to live.

'But we are fine. I mean, of course we're adjusting, but we're okay. Elijah is okay.' Leah wasn't sure at what point she had interrupted Jane, but she was reaffirming the statement for herself.

'What about his schooling? He should be there today.'

'It's the last week of term. This is just temporary until I find the money to pay for his private school fees.'

Jane peered over the top of her glasses and paused to write notes. She then lifted herself from the sofa. 'Do you mind?'

Leah wasn't sure what she meant but she nodded anyway. Jane looked around and opened the door to the bathroom and Leah's bedroom. She walked over to the window and peered around the kitchen. Jane wrote more notes.

'Okay, well, I'm going to be off now. I will see you next week.'

'Why? I just told you we are perfectly fine.'

'It's mandatory that your child is in school, Ophelia, and also that I have sufficient evidence of your wellbeing in order to close the case.'

'And what if I can't get him back into his school?'

'Are you removing Elijah from the school system?'

'I can't afford it at the moment –'

'Are you planning on providing Elijah's education through home-schooling?'

'No, I...'

'Then I think it's necessary I come back next week. You'll also need to clean the flat. It poses a health and safety risk since the main fire escape route is blocked and the cleanliness, – it isn't conducive to having a young child in here.'

Leah swallowed hard. The blood vessels tightened in her head and feeling dizzy, she perched on the end of the sofa.

'If you need me in the meantime, please call me. If you want extra support, we also provide services to help people in your situation.'

My situation, Leah thought. Jane saw herself out and Leah stared at her situation. Her reflection in the dull TV screen, her unwashed hair, her pyjamas and robe. The clock ticking behind her chimed as it struck one o'clock. Her baby was at home, behind a cheap door in a pokey bedroom, whilst his friends were at school in their blazers, learning to be future leaders. The guilt felt like acid in her blood, exacerbated by the thought of what Matthew would think if he saw them now. What he had left them to. How she was nothing by herself. The door unclicked as Elijah opened it and Leah turned her face to the side, quickly rubbing the tears off her cheeks.

'Are you okay, mummy?' Elijah said, shuffling over and wrapping his arms round her.

'Yes darling, everything is fine. Mummy just needs to sort some things out.'

'I'll help you, mummy.'

Leah sat there holding Elijah. She pressed him so tightly, realising that maybe she wanted him to be with her just so she wasn't on her own. Plus, her anxiety peaked every time he left her sight since Matthew went. What if it happened to him? Could it be hereditary? Her heart weakened as the world and its possible dangers played out in her head. Every possibility of what could go wrong exhausted her. Now all her suffocating had led to her being the reason she could lose him. She stood up and released him from her grip. She had to make a change. And just as she was about to begin cleaning, she remembered she was due to help her neighbour find the Town Hall. She had asked her to be there in the morning and she had completely forgotten. If she had been there like she said she would, she wouldn't have been there when the social worker came.

'Elijah, get dressed. We need to take our neighbour somewhere.'

She threw on some clothes and headed out the door, buttoning up Elijah's jacket as they went, despite the sun streaming through the window. You can't be too careful, thought Leah, ignoring his fingers trying to take over doing up his buttons and the fact that he kept telling her that he was perfectly capable of doing it himself. Instead, Leah snapped them into place one by one, distressed by the clamping feeling that was taking hold of her gut as she reran scenarios of her mother's betrayal in her head. She knew they didn't always agree. It had started off in secondary school and stopped briefly as she became everything her mum wanted her to be. She had almost graduated medical school and was close to becoming the daughter her mum had always dreamed of. But when she met Matthew, it began again. He didn't fit. As soon as she began to oppose her mother's wishes, the battle resumed. She clipped Elijah's last button up to his chin and rushed down the stairwell, before knocking on Reem's door.

~ *Reem* ~

Reem woke up at *fajr*. It was almost light by the time she had finished and was still kneeling on the prayer mat facing the window. She had her hands cupped to the sky, and asked Allah to help her find a way to Adar. It was still the early hours of the morning since dawn broke a lot earlier than it ever had back home, but Reem couldn't go back to sleep. She imagined all the possibilities of the day, the fact that she was beginning an official search for him, that others would be helping her. She laid down on her prayer mat and tried to imagine what was going to happen, how it would work. Then, a creeping doubt set in. What if Leah didn't come? As the city woke up beneath her, she saw how hard it would be for her to navigate.

To take her mind off the hours that needed to pass before Leah arrived, she unwrapped her parcels and polished them up, displaying them underneath the window. She turned around and saw her flat. Empty except for those belongings and a few clothes they had donated to her when she left the temporary accommodation she was housed in before. She remembered what it was like, sleeping in a room full of strangers. How at night, the air in the room sank into a pit of salty tears, nervous sweat and fear as people's nightmares came to life in the shadows. The sparseness of the flat made her feel better. Like everything was stripped bare and there was nothing hiding in it. The walls were plain to see; there was no clutter, no memories, no bloodstains. Just a blank canvas.

Reem didn't want to think about it anymore. She headed to the kitchen and switched on the oven, despite it being six in the morning. She used the last of her eggs and had only a thin cube of butter, so made the rest up with oil and added flour and desiccated coconut. She baked the cake in the oven and stirred up sugar to make a sweet syrup for the top. Her mum used to make it at least once a week and it was one of her favourites. It was Adar's favourite. She wouldn't have been so frivolous with her ingredients, or with her limited funds, if it wasn't for today being different to every other day. Today was the day she had been waiting for since the day she woke up to find Adar gone. It felt like the days had stretched into one another and with each one that passed, the distance between her and Adar had become greater. Today, she was going to shorten that distance. She was going to make positive steps to find him and it wouldn't be long until they were celebrating together. She didn't want to get too ahead of herself, but he could be coming back with them today. It could happen.

Reem showered and dressed for the occasion. She tucked her long, rich brown hair behind her neck, trying to cover the scar that ran down the left side of it. By the time the cake had baked and was almost cooled on the side, it was eight o'clock. By ten, there was still no sign of Leah. Reem began to despair. She didn't want to try and attempt to go herself. She paced the room and pressed her ear to the door, stood silently waiting to hear movement outside. She desperately wanted to hear Leah's voice or hear Elijah bounding over and hammering the door with his little fist. She would play it cool, like she had almost forgotten it was the day she was going to find her brother *in'shaa'Allah*. By midday the excitement had worn off and she cried a little on the sofa, flicking through the news channels, not listening to anything that was being reported. So, when the knock did come, she jumped. She grabbed the cake tin and ran to the door, realising she had been wearing her coat and shoes all morning.

Reem followed Leah through the paved streets, down steps into underground stations and back up to the fresh air. She tried to remember where they went, which direction they took, what the train stations were called, but it was too hectic. Reem hadn't seen this many people together in all her life. It took up most of her concentration to stay by Leah and not lose her in the crowds.

Elijah seemed used to it. He even led the way in parts. Reem could tell he had been raised in the city and was impressed at how easily he found himself there, amongst what seemed to her like hundreds of strangers.

'It's this one,' Elijah said, grabbing her hand and gearing up to push his way through to the doors. They walked up the steps together and through the streets, stopping at a reddish brown brick building, stacked up over three storeys with small rectangular windows. It looked almost prison-like. Only a few trees broke up the imposing footprint of the large building in front of her. A simple 'Town Hall' sign with what looked like a Royal badge on the front made the building seem too official, and for a moment, she didn't want to go in.

Inside, it was easier to navigate. Signs led to different parts of the building. A 'Refugees Welcome' sign pointed to a few makeshift stands in a main hall area where some staff with name badges sat at tables, with a long queue of people behind them.

'I think you have to go there. They will help you,' said Leah, gesturing to the end of the long line.

'What if I can't read it?'

'Don't worry, I'll come over if you need me to,' said Leah, looking at the clock up on the wall. 'It shouldn't take too long.'

Reem queued in the line, unavoidably hearing the plight of those before her. People had lost children, parents – sometimes entire families were unaccounted for.

Reem's memory revisited her waking up on the shore. There was no one else there. Then the feeling of the water came back to her, suddenly soaking her clothes, the cold seeping through.

'Next.'

Reem saw Leah had sat a few chairs down from the desks, just out of earshot. Leah must have thought Reem was beckoning her to come over as she joined her immediately and began to talk on her behalf.

'This is Reem. She's lost her brother and she was told to come here to give you her details so that you can help to find him. Maybe put him on the Missing Persons file.'

'Okay, I will need your full name, including your family name and your missing brother's name, and any photos you may have.'

Leah filled out the forms as Reem told her as much as she could. They had his age, name, physical description, but no photograph. Reem saw the size of the file that his details were put into. Leah slipped and dropped the file, the pages flicking past Reem's eyes, a mass of photographs of missing men, women and children staring up at her.

'We have procedures for this, don't worry. We work closely with other councils and most missing persons eventually come forward and give their names, so we can reunite family members.'

Reem felt hopeless. She didn't know what she had imagined this morning. Rooms of uncollected children waiting to be called forward? Had she thought that Adar would wind up in the same borough of London, even be in the capital itself? She was too hot in her best coat. She took it off, knowing she didn't need to wear it anymore. The cake in her bag had gone cold. She would give the rest to Elijah. The thought of eating it herself made her feel guilty.

Reem watched as Leah and Elijah waved from the Tube. Leah had her hand on Elijah's shoulder and Reem wondered if she knew how blessed she was to be with him. If she knew what it felt like to have someone you love, right there in front of you. Never knowing the fear or the gaping hole that losing them would leave in you. Reem walked the short distance from the station to home, appreciating the space she needed to allow herself to cry without Elijah seeing her.

She closed the door behind her and curled up in front of the window. All the hope from the morning had burnt away. She took the cake tin out, having forgotten to give it to Elijah, and a bunch of leaflets from the Town Hall fell out onto the floor. There was a local community centre only five minutes away which was also a mosque. The centre also hosted free English classes. A mosque was just what she needed, she thought. If anyone could help her, it was Allah. She reminded herself to be patient, that Adar belonged to God and when the time was right, they would be reunited.

~ Leah ~

Leah left Reem on the last underground stop before home and made sure she knew the direction to take to get back to the building. She and Elijah stayed on the Tube. She couldn't wait any longer before confronting her parents. She knew it must have been her mum who had reported her to social services. Leah was so angry that she could stoop so low. It was too far, even for her. Her mum knew the only thing she had left was Elijah, yet she still tried to get him taken away.

She hammered on the door. 'Mum, open this door now!' she shouted, unable to contain herself.

'Stop making such a racket, Ophelia. What if the neighbours hear?' her mum said through the door, as she tried to open it. 'What on earth has happened?'

'Don't act like you don't know.'

Barbara began ushering her in, and pulling Elijah inside. 'Go and play, sweetheart, your old toys are in the cabin in the back of the garden.' Leah saw her mum was overdressed for a dismal weekday afternoon. Her hair was distinctly old-fashioned. Cut around her head to give her volume, she had kept it short to her neck when it started thinning and she hadn't changed the hairstyle since. Leah noticed it looked redder, like she had dyed it only recently. It didn't suit her, she thought. It brought out the redness in her plump cheeks and looked too rich against her light eyebrows.

Leah held it in as Elijah walked out the back. The house looked bigger than she remembered it. It wasn't particularly bright considering it was a warm summer's day, but it definitely felt different. Wooden doors were flung open, allowing the ground floor to become almost one open space. She noticed the thick, gold embossed wallpaper, the heavy twelve-seater table, the crystal chandeliers, the engraved skirting boards. The newly purchased matching furniture sets in the lounge framed an imported handmade Chinese table. That alone must have been worth more than six months of her rent.

With Elijah out of earshot, Leah shouted, 'You called the government on me to tell them I can't look after my own child!'

'Now calm down, Ophelia, I –'

'Do you know what that felt like for Elijah? After everything he's been through? What on earth is wrong with you? You redecorate with all this expensive junk, call the social on your grandson – is that what your days have turned into?' Leah threw down her phone and it smashed on the new Chinese table.

Phillip had come down from his office. 'What's all this noise?' he said, standing halfway down the stairs, scratching where his once thick head of hair was. Leah noticed it was now peppered grey and white, making his face look paler than usual.

'Did you know about this, daddy?' Leah said, her voice changing when she saw how much weight he seemed to have lost since she saw him last. His trousers bunched up around his waist and his shirt seemed to hang off his shoulders, jutting out sharply from his neck.

Phillip shot a glare at Barbara. 'You didn't, Barbara?'

Barbara paused. 'Of course not.'

'Why didn't you say it straight away then if you really didn't? You know if you did or not. It's just sick. As if I haven't lost enough.'

Leah burst out crying. 'Elijah, come,' she called out into the garden, but he hadn't heard her. He was too busy playing, motoring one of his bikes around the neatly manicured lawn.

'Let him play,' her dad said, 'it isn't easy for him, living where you have chosen.'

'Chosen? I couldn't afford anywhere else.'

'You could have afforded it if you hadn't dropped out of your hospital placement.'

'Did you ever consider that maybe I didn't want to be a doctor? That I wasn't very good at it?'

'You had nearly graduated, Leah. Your exam scores were one of the highest in your class.'

'Being a doctor isn't about grades. People die, you know. People you have a duty to take care of.'

'Ophelia, Matthew wasn't your fault. You have to let it go.'

Leah darted away from them both, rushing towards the back door.

'Elijah,' she shouted, but he was too far to hear.

'Let him play, and you sit down with us. Please, sit with us, have some tea. We can talk about this,' her dad said, following her frantic movements around the dining room.

'I am not staying another minute.'

Leah ran out onto the street and slammed the door behind her. The tears ran freely. She didn't have Elijah with her to tamper them, because usually she played at being strong for him. But here in her old street, where she would walk him to school, and planned to raise him in the wide, tree-lined suburban streets, dreaming of what he could become, she felt the distance between where she now lived and here – her old home. It was a space she didn't know how to fill.

She could barely see where she was going when she bumped into Emily Alcott. Emily lived in one of the most expensive houses on the street. She was friends with her since secondary school, but Leah hadn't seen her lately. Emily looked thinner than usual, which was hard for Leah to imagine considering she had only ever had a size eight frame. Her hair was bleached bright platinum blonde and the diamond on her engagement finger covered most of her wedding band. Leah coarsely rubbed away her tears and pulled her creased blouse down so it didn't look so dishevelled, but she doubted that helped.

'Leah! I haven't seen you in so long.'

'Yes, I know. It's been a while. You look well, though,' Leah said, composing herself.

'You too, you too,' Emily said, her eyes widening in surprise as she looked her over.

Leah was conscious that she hadn't dyed her hair in weeks, her nails were chewed, and her clothes were worn straight from the boxes.

'Congratulations on the wedding and the house move.'

'Ah, thank you darling, such a shame you couldn't make it. It was glorious. But of course, the Caribbean is! Ray was such a darling. But it's back to it now and I'm so busy, you wouldn't believe it.' Emily paused, rattling her car keys between her fingers. 'You aren't working at the minute, are you?'

Leah shook her head. She didn't know what was coming next, but anything that focused the conversation on Emily's life rather than her own suited her. The last thing Leah wanted to do was to talk to her about the year she had just had.

chapter 4

~ *Leah* ~

The garden was on the eighth floor, a couple of flights from their apartment. It was an open courtyard with high railings around the edges, so it was at least safer than Leah had first expected when Mo had told her about it. A small crowd of people stopped talking and turned to look at her almost in unison. They fell silent as they gazed up and down at her. She felt exposed, like she didn't belong. Awkwardly, she turned and headed straight for the crates that were around the edges of the courtyard. They had been stacked into composting beds, one on top of another like steps, filled with soil. Leah was surprised to see the variety of what was growing. Handwritten labels showed what vegetables grew, and the soil beds were sectioned for root vegetables, beans and bulbs.

On the other side of the square courtyard, a living wall was in progress. Patches of moss climbed its surface and bamboo and sunflowers towered next to it, creating a green seating area where a painted sign saying 'Retreat' was stuck into a plant pot in the ground.

Leah didn't usually consider invitations for events and groups such as the Garden Club, but Elijah really wanted to go. He told her that he was convinced there were bones and treasures to be found under the soil and he reminded her of how he would spend their weekends in the garden with his dad. How they had found treasure once. Of course, Leah knew that it was treasure they had planted themselves, and she wanted to tell Elijah that discoveries of ancient history were not discovered in compost bags, but since she didn't want to fracture his hopes, she agreed immediately. Plus, he seemed to love Mo and wanted to go wherever he went.

'Good to see you, Elijah,' said Mo, high-fiving him as he ran towards him.

Leah felt the smack of their two hands like a thump in her side. She could never be that person he wanted to be next to. It was as if everyone else understood him more than she did. She wondered if it was because he blamed her too. After all, how does an almost qualified doctor not spot the signs of heart failure?

'Yo Mo!' Elijah replied.

Leah hadn't heard him say that before... Would he be an entirely different boy growing up here? What would they think when school started again and he was talking like that? She pushed the feelings down and swallowed them hard. She walked over to Mo to say hi, but he had already turned his face away and was guiding Elijah to a rectangular sand bed on the ground framed by bits of old timber, where old paintbrushes and soft rubber shovels were lying in the sand.

'Now here is where the palaeontologists work.'

Elijah jumped onto it and started dusting away at the sand and soil. Leah had the feeling Mo was avoiding her again so she stood at the side watching Elijah dig and tried to ignore the stares burning into her back. She gazed out of the view over the top of the railings. This part of London looked so different to what she was used to. But just beyond the tower blocks and old cement buildings, the iconic buildings rose into the sky – a different part of the city, one she wanted Elijah to occupy one day.

Leah looked around the garden courtyard, trying to take it all in. Nidal was next to him, his hands tucked into a sports jacket that he was wearing over his white robe. Mo stood out in his short ankle-length trousers, a plain white T-shirt and his trademark white cap that Leah hadn't seen him without. People spoke to one another, changing languages effortlessly between English and what Leah assumed to be their native tongue. She walked over to the table where an array of trays and Tupperware boxes were holding freshly prepared food that she hadn't seen before. Syrup-coated balls of pastry sat in Japanese style soup bowls, samosas and other unidentifiable pastries, crisp and golden, were arranged in patterns around a circular crystal effect serving plate. The aromas of spices and sugar mixed together in the air, making Leah hungry. She leant forward and took a bite of the hot samosas filled with spices she couldn't determine and fresh vegetables ground into a paste. She popped a pastry ball in afterwards and savoured the super-sweet syrup as it stuck to her tongue. Her neighbours could cook, she thought.

Over in the corner of the garden, Leah watched as Harold watered the flower pots by the wall. He was hunched over so the curve in his back looked more prominent and forced Leah to straighten hers automatically.

A loud voice broke her daydreaming.

'Leah, ain't it?'

Leah turned around, briefly recognising the tall, well-built guy in front of her. He was Mo's brother, Nidal. He had helped move her sofa up to her apartment the day she moved in. The thought of her bringing the sofa here made her cringe.

'Yes... Yes, it is.'

'We're gonna get together to talk about stuff that affects all the residents. You in?'

'I, erm... what is it about? I'm not planning on living here for very long.'

'It's the new cladding they've put on the outside of the building. There's reports that it ain't safe.'

'Why not?'

'The material they use. It's cheaper than some other stuff and some of the residents are in talks with the council about changing it, so we're trying to get some support. It don't matter how long you're here for though. A signature is a signature.'

Leah nodded, although the frown that crept into her forehead when she was made to do things she didn't really want to do was harder to hide.

'It starts in ten,' Nidal said, gesturing to the group starting to gather at the Retreat corner.

At the entrance, the door started rattling. Leah looked over and saw Reem through the glass. Leah went over, relieved she had someone there that she felt familiar with. Reem was struggling to find the button to press that opened the door onto the courtyard.

'Press the button,' Leah mouthed through the door, pointing her finger to where it was.

She saw Reem blush and open the door.

'Thank you.'

'No problem, it's nice to see you here. Elijah is here too but he isn't interested in me, he's digging for bones. Oh, and they have a meeting going on. I'm not sure what it's about but apparently it involves us all.'

'I am here for that. Mo invited me.'

Leah took a sharp intake of breath and just as Reem opened her mouth to speak, they heard Mo calling them over.

'Now that we're all here, I want to say thanks for coming. It's important we stick together,' Mo said.

Leah watched him. His voice was smooth but his mannerisms, the way his hands moved and fidgeted as he spoke, showed a hint of vulnerability.

'Before we get started, we have some new faces here today, so Leah, if you want to start by introducing yourself, we'll then go round and ask everyone to tell you a bit about themselves too.'

Leah was caught completely off guard. She stood up a little from her chair, then decided sitting was better. She crossed her legs and cleared her throat.

'I'm Leah. I have just moved in with my son, Elijah.'

'Okay, what do you do, Leah?' Mo asked encouragingly.

'Nothing. At the moment. I mean.'

A silence fell upon the group. Leah continued, 'I like gardening. I used to garden back when I had a home. I mean a house. Bees. I was good at keeping bees.'

'I would love a beehive up here. Our own honey. Can you do one?' Brianna asked.

'Let's add that to the list of things to look at,' Mo said, not giving Leah time to modestly decline. He moved straight on. 'Reem?'

Leah watched Reem stand up awkwardly.

'*Salam*, I'm Reem. From Syria.'

Reem sat down straight after, so Mo moved on.

'Okay thanks. Bill, you go next.'

'I'm Bill, a retired bricky, and I spend my time paintin' now. Mostly outsides of buildins. Nothin' famous like, just what I fancy.'

'Chantelle here, and this is my sis, Brianna. I don't call myself a waitress cos that's temporary. I'm just doing it til my music takes off, so you all can download my tunes via my new website...www.chantyrhymes –'

'Thanks for that Chantelle, as always, no intro needed.'

Leah learnt that the two sisters flat-shared up on the sixteenth floor. They looked completely different. The eldest one by eleven months, Chantelle, had long hair extensions in and perfectly manicured nails that were painted in bright coral, with make-up to match.

Her sister, Brianna, wore her hair in natural curls that almost reached the tops of her shoulders. She wore black-rimmed glasses and no make-up. Her college bag rested by her feet, sagging at the sides from being stuffed with books and exam timetables that were poking out of the top. Brianna wore jeans and a thin jumper with a colourful patterned band around her head, whilst Chantelle's outfit seemed to be made of multi-coloured cotton fabric billowing out against the backdrop of the grey high-rise buildings and sky. Leah marvelled at how different they looked but how their actions were almost identical. They crossed their legs in the same direction, gasped at the same time, opened their mouths to speak at the same time and pursed their lips when they didn't like something.

'Thanks guys, so for today. First on the agenda is the cladding. Then anything else you all want to add or need help with,' Mo said. 'We've all heard about the cladding they've put on and we aren't saying it don't look nice, but there's been reports that it ain't safe.'

'Not safe – they may as well have stuck cotton wool on the outside. That stuff will light up like a match. I may be retired but I know that from my buildin' days.'

Bill sat back, visibly relieved that he had let if off his chest and puffed up from his obvious technical knowledge.

'Thanks, Bill. That's why we're campaigning. Now you all got the letters?'

'Nah, I ain't got no letter,' Nidal said.

'Me neither, bruv.'

Leah recognised the second speaker as Nidal's mate, Ali, who was also there on moving day. They looked restless. Mo had probably dragged them there, Leah thought to herself with a smile broadening her face.

'I have some more. Please take one when you leave and add your signature to the list.'

Mo glanced over at Leah. Leah looked at Reem. Her eyes scanning the floor, as though she had lost something.

'Reem, are you okay?'

Reem looked up.

'Yes. Yes. I was thinking about something. The signs – I don't know if I read them right.'

'What did you read?'

'If there is a fire, you must stay in your flat.'

Leah nodded before adding, 'Yes, that's what I read. It doesn't sound right to me. But I guess they know what they're doing.'

'Should I ask?'

'Let's put that on the letter. Maybe Mo can bring it up?'

'Yes, okay.'

'Don't look so worried, Reem. It's unlikely it will ever happen. Just one of those things you need to be cautious about.'

Leah looked at her, waiting for confirmation, but it never came. Instead her face looked sunken as though things hadn't always worked out how they should for her. Leah remembered her brother.

'Any news on Adar?'

'Nothing. No sign.'

Leah stayed silent as though she had somehow made her feel worse. She was relieved when Elijah bounded over.

'I've found dinosaur bones.'

Leah smiled. 'Wow, where?'

'In the sand. Quick, come and look, Reem.'

Leah stood up the moment he had said it and needed a few minutes to adjust to the fact that he was pulling Reem up to go and see it. Leah looked at Reem. The look had been replaced by a gentle smile, and the two left her behind to listen to the rest of the meeting.

'Does anyone have anything else the community can help with?'

Leah's mind raced. Could they help with the social worker visits from Jane? She knew Jane visited at least one more person in the building, but she was too embarrassed to actually bring it up. What would they think of her, she wondered.

'I'm reporting on local stories so if anyone has any ideas let me know,' Nidal said.

'Oh yeah, you only write fluff so you don't stand out too much,' Chantelle said.

Nidal stepped forward, his body tensed. 'How do you know?'

'I haven't been living under a rock. I follow your blog. Usually read it at bed time, sends me sleep!' She laughed.

'Chill, bruv, she's windin' you up and you takin' the bait every time,' Ali said, pushing him down.

'Chantelle. Please,' Brianna said, trying to tug her sister down into her chair whilst straining to keep her voice low, and trying to lighten up how she felt by flickering a smile to the rest of the group. 'I follow it too, Nidal, and it's interesting and informative,' she said, in such a matter-of-fact way that Chantelle didn't know how to respond.

'Okay, let's move on. I will be arranging a Big Iftar and will need help with that,' Mo broke in, giving the meeting a much needed change of tone.

'What is a Big Iftar?' Leah asked.

'We do it every year,' Bill said, without giving any more information.

'In Ramadan, Muslims like myself, Nidal, Ali...' he paused. 'Reem as well. We all fast during the day and when the sun sets we break our fast by eating and drinking.'

'So, where are you guys from?' Leah said, gesturing to the men he had just mentioned. No one spoke, so Leah carried on, 'Like Reem, she is from Syria, so...'

'We are British,' Nidal said simply. 'You don't have to be from anywhere to be Muslim.'

Mo tapped him on the shoulder and he sat down. 'Thanks, bro. Yep, anyone can choose to be Muslim. There's a large Muslim population in our community and we all come from loads of different places.' He turned to Leah. 'Each year, we arrange a Big Iftar – they happen all over London and the UK. It's where we get everyone together to eat at sundown.'

'Can anyone come?'

'Yes, that's the idea. Everyone comes together regardless of what they believe. It's a community thing, really.'

Mo paused. There were no more questions so he wrapped it up. 'So if that's all. Same time next week. Thanks, guys.'

Leah went to collect Elijah and say bye to Reem.

Reem hung around the door, then turned back and said to Leah, 'I will see you later. I need to talk to the one who writes. I think he can help.'

~ Reem ~

'You are looking for news stories?' Reem asked inquisitively as Nidal sat on the chair, texting on his phone.

'Yeah, I always need things to write about,' he said, looking up at her and tucking his phone into his pocket.

'Who do you write for?'

'It's a pretty new news site. Trying to develop into one that only tells the truth. No headlines made up to gain more readers or things like that. No fake news.' He pulled out a chair and gestured to Reem to sit down.

Reem paused as though considering something. 'What if I could tell you things that are happening to people that not many people know about?'

'Sure, tell me. I'll jot it down if that's okay?' Nidal said, pulling out a crumpled notebook and pen from his pocket.

'That would be good.'

Reem began when the other members of the gardening club had left. Mo was down the other side of the garden, watering the plants, but she didn't mind him being there. She told Nidal how she believed Adar was taken on the night they arrived. She remembers some things from her arrival. Not much – mostly snapshots, images, sometimes a smell – would reboot her memory but so far it wasn't clear. She remembered being on the boat with at least one hundred other people, who had sold everything for the last chance to escape the war that had crippled the country.

She told Nidal about how she thought she saw Adar's face in the back of a lorry. It had a black-painted back, with two long metal locks that clamped it shut. Painted on it, a sticker read 'Funnel Logistics'.

'Maybe you could tell people about this. Make them see?'

Reem could tell by the look in Nidal's eyes that it wasn't that easy.

'I need evidence,' Nidal said, in such a matter-of-fact way that Reem physically withdrew from him.

'You don't believe me?'

'I ain't saying I don't believe you, but I can't just write what I want.'

Reem stood up, hurt and exposed. She had shared so much in the hope that he could help, but he hadn't even believed her.

'Are you okay, Reem?' Mo said, appearing in between them, taking off his muddy garden gloves. Reem saw him glare at his brother.

'Don't look at me like that. I'm sorry I can't help, but I don't know what you expect me to do?' Neither of them was sure who Nidal's question was directed at, so he continued, 'I need more, Reem. I can't just go on this. It ain't enough.'

'But I know something terrible has happened. I feel it.'

'I wish I could do something but...' Nidal said, standing up and stuffing his notebook back into his pocket. 'Don't look at me like that, bro.'

'I'm not,' Mo protested.

'Whatever, I'm off. Sorry if I made it worse and everything, yeah. But I didn't mean to.'

'Don't go.'

Nidal waved his hand in the air as he walked off and let the door close behind him.

Mo stood shifting his weight on both of his feet.

'We should go. I'll walk you home.'

Mo threw his gloves on the chair while patting down the sides of his hair that were beginning to curl underneath his sweat. Reem looked at him. He reminded her of an old friend back home. He was a childhood friend who lived next door and they had grown up together. His name was Mahmoud. There was something about Mo's mannerisms that reminded her of him, and she realised that it must have been the reason she connected with Mo immediately. He tried to model his behaviour on the Prophet Muhammad. Reem recognised it in how he would lower his gaze when she was talking to him. She saw it in how he tried to help others, volunteered for things, tried to make a difference. So when he didn't want to be alone with a woman he wasn't related or married to, she understood why. He didn't want to break the traditions of his faith.

Mahmoud was the same. When they grew older, he started avoiding her. At first, she was hurt by his sudden withdrawal but when he had left, she knew why he was doing it and felt foolish for not spotting it earlier. This small link between her home and here, no matter how tentative, how fragile, was enough to remind her that life still existed and carried on despite changes and shifts. That there were parts of people's mannerisms, their behaviours, that lived on in others. It gave her an unexpected contentment.

When Reem arrived home, she felt less troubled. There was something about offloading to Nidal, the ease with Mo, that made her feel as if her arrival there wasn't just the end of her past, but the beginning of a different future.

Reem hadn't been home long before she heard someone at the door. She still wasn't used to how the building seemed to breathe and heave as if it was alive, as though at any moment it could burst under the seams of all the lives it was trying to hold in. Knocks and bangs from other apartments permeated her walls. Taps running, toilets being flushed, footsteps outside in the hallway, all seemed to reverberate on her floor as if there were beings living amongst her, unseen. The knocks came again but this time she recognised them. She had become used to the sound of his little tapping knock against the door.

Elijah would come in and walk straight over to the now unwrapped pieces that lay under a blanket on the table. Reem watched as Elijah picked up the old gold coin and turned it towards the light. He took out his pyrite and lay it on the table next to it. His own treasure mixing with hers. She would tell him about where it had come from, even though she knew he couldn't always understand her broken English. She told Elijah all the stories of where she lived, in a landscape wildly different from here. He sat with her and the two of them were transported out of the thin walls of the apartment, across oceans, to a place that only existed in their imaginations.

Her words sometimes failed her in this language despite her mind bursting with an array of colours and scenes; images of the historical souks packed with antiques, handmade clothes, silks. Sights she had seen every day when meandering through the town to pick up things for her mother, weaving through the ancient part of the city that effortlessly blended with the new, creating a link between the past and present.

Reem wanted to hold on to what had made her and by sharing them with Elijah it created stories for him and preserved hers – the place she had come from. She told him about the sound of the *athan* filling the skies, of the bright morning sun burning away the mist and leaving behind the hot air, and the smell of *oud* as the city woke up. She wanted to tell him about her mother's rice and fish and how the caramelised onions tasted on top. How her mother would laugh and spend hours up through the evenings with her sisters, twisting grapevine leaves stuffed with rice and loading them into a pot to feed the family for days. How her father would wear his cream *kandura* after work, sipping Arabic coffee in the shade, before walking to the prayers at the mosque where he would stay until after dusk. The stories brought alive images of Reem's mother tending to the fruits in the garden, and sometimes she could close her eyes and remember them. Peaceful and happy, when there was no threat, nothing to frighten her, just quiet skies with the twittering of birds as they rustled in the twigs of the pomegranate tree.

'Daddy gave me this,' Elijah said, dusting off his pyrite. 'Just before – it happened.'

'Is that why you love it so much?'

'I guess so.' Elijah stopped. He even held his breath so Reem stayed quiet, knowing he had more to tell. 'I think that's why I like digging to find old things.'

'Why?'

Elijah placed it down and picked up the gold coin in Reem's collection. 'Do you think there is only treasure underneath the earth?'

'No. Not just in the earth. I think the real treasure is waiting for us above the skies.'

'Like in heaven, you mean?'

'Yes, Elijah, that's just what I mean.' Reem paused for a minute, unsure of which direction to go. 'You know, in the book I have read about heaven, it says that when the world ends, all the treasures and gold and jewels hiding in the earth will be thrown up to the surface.'

Elijah's face lit up. 'Wow, will I get to see it all? I wonder how much there is and where it will be?'

Reem laughed. 'I don't know, but imagine if it is all there for us, it can't be worth as much as we think.'

'I hope daddy has found it.'

Reem smiled and stroked his hair. She was lost for words.

'I was there when he... when he...'

Reem stayed silent, allowing him to find his own way of expressing it.

'He died. It was so fast. Like he was talking to me, and then...'

Reem held him close as he sobbed. There was nothing else she could say. Just being there was enough. She knew, and she would never tell him. She wouldn't tell Elijah the last time she had seen life snatched away in a flash of red. Elijah would never know the last time she had seen the *souk*. How she was there in the aftermath, on the blood-stained streets where the broken rubble and burnt canopies that once covered glittering tables were hung, now destroyed and empty. Where smashed shards of deep violet glass and gold littered the floor. The mosque's dome that once anchored together the two parts of the city, now sunk below the walls. Its dome deflated, sagging down under the weight of the broken walls. She remembered how upset her mother was when she didn't return home after the bombing but Reem was in shock. The sound made her ears bleed. All around her a stunned silence in the shattering aftermath of the explosion. Mannequin legs and arms were detached, strewn all over the stone. Ripped apart by the force of the blast. When her hearing came back to her, she wished it hadn't. The air filled with screams of pain. And it was the first time that Reem disappeared into her own world.

Desperate to piece things back together, she gathered what she could and stuffed it into her bag. She stayed there, gathering mosaics, pieces from the mosque walls. Fragments of the mosque walls that were decorated with calligraphy from verses of the Qur'an were stuffed inside. Her bag was overloaded. She stumbled home, past more detached limbs. Her neck and shoulder were burnt from the fire, but she couldn't feel it. The only thing that kept her legs moving forward, moving past hands that grappled at her feet, from pleas of the dying to help, was the fact that she was carrying her past with her. Towns of the past, their history on her back.

It was only during her recovery, when the images returned, that she realised the horror of what her eyes had failed to see at the time. There had never been any mannequins back at the *souk*.

chapter 5

~ *Leah* ~

Leah had noticed that Elijah was spending a lot of time with Reem, so when the invitation came from Emily to join them for a picnic in Wandsworth to watch the Oxford and Cambridge boat race, she decided that it would be a good idea for them all to go together.

She was also tired of being in the apartment. She donated half of her stuff, so all that was left was the essentials she and Elijah needed. That way, it became easier to stay on top of the housework and there was no room for extras in her small apartment. It actually made her feel a little bit better to have removed so much of her old life.

She called Mo to help fix the curtain. The doorbell rang and Leah quickly smudged on some lip balm, checking herself over in the mirror. She opened the door, but no one was there.

'Hello,' she called, seeing that Mo and Nidal were stood a few feet down.

'Is it okay to come in?'

'Yes, of course, come in,' she said.

The two of them walked in, Nidal with a ladder under his arm.

'Do you want tea or anything?' Leah asked.

'No, we're fine,' said Mo, nipping back out to fetch a drill and leaving the door wide open.

'Let me close the door.'

'Nah, leave it, we won't be a minute,' Nidal said, steadying the ladder as Mo climbed up it.

The drill made short work of the wall and the curtains were soon rehung. Leah had found some pale green ones with big leaves on them and blossoming flowers.

'Here, hang these instead,' she said, dragging them out of the box and chucking the old ones to the side. They brighten the place up, she thought, pleased that she had found them as she was sifting through her things.

'Where's the little man?' Mo asked, stacking away the screws.

'He's at Reem's. I'm actually on my way there now. We're heading down to Wandsworth to see the boat race. Do you two fancy joining us?'

'Thanks, but it ain't really my scene,' said Nidal.

'I have some hours to do for work this afternoon so I can't either,' Mo said.

'Oh.' Leah packed up the picnic basket, trying not to look disappointed.

Leah straightened herself out and thanked them again as they left to go back up to their apartment. She went to Reem's, trying to balance the picnic basket as she knocked on the door.

'Elijah, Reem, it's me!'

Reem opened the door and Leah launched into her speech. 'I thought you would feel better if you got out and headed with me and a couple of friends to the riverside today. I won't take no for an answer. The fresh air will do you good.'

'Come in, come in. But you two go. I don't really want to.'

'Oh please come, it won't be the same without you. Plus, I made a picnic. And it's out of the city a bit. I think you'll enjoy it.'

Reem gave in and went to her room to change, leaving Leah to watch Elijah.

'How are you, darling? Have you had fun? What did you two do?'

'We played games and told stories,' said Elijah, as Leah looked around. She couldn't see any toys or games out. Just some old pieces of junk on the side.

Reem came out, swamped in an oversized flowing kimono that was too long for her petite arms and hung below her knees.

'Are you sure you won't be too hot in that?' Leah said.

Reem disagreed and they headed out to meet Elijah who was playing on the grass downstairs. Leah noticed how he ran straight to Reem, talking to her erratically about the discovery he had made in the patches of soil around the edges of the building.

'Leave Reem alone, Elijah. You're talking too fast for her to understand.'

Elijah stopped talking and hooked his hand under Reem's arm. Leah left him to it, despite the voice in her head complaining that he never walked that close to her, his own mum, yet this new girl had won his affection so easily.

Leah carried the beach bag packed with the things for the day. It was warm and the sky was a bright cloudless blue. She led the way, taking a backseat to Elijah and Reem's own small space. She tried to break in every now and then with comments on dinosaur bones or stories of buried treasure that she thought would pique his interest, but her comments always came off strange, childish. Leah decided to concentrate on the sounds of the reliable machinery of the train taking them to their destination. The orderly lines of the map, the inner workings of the engines, running smoothly along predestined routes. Leah realised that she could never bridge the gap into his world and see what he saw. She only saw what was there. What could be seen or touched or felt. She couldn't see past the hard walls, the floor beneath her feet. Elijah's world existed in the spaces in between. He filled it with the workings of his imagination, with all the possibilities that could be there.

Down by the river bank, her old friends had already arrived and were sat at a perfect spot to watch the rowers pass. There was a wide strip of muddy bank that went down from the pavement, situated at a higher elevation, away from the shoreline and protected by white fence that sectioned off the front of the tavern. They had set up parasols and collapsible tables and chairs under the shade on a large, woven bamboo picnic mat. There were drinks on ice, plates, bowls and cutlery strapped into large hampers prefilled with a variety of food. Some of the wives were sitting in the Tavern above the banks. They had set themselves up to watch the race via the wide TV screens inside the pub. She scanned the faces and couldn't find Emily among them.

Leah rushed forward to join them, relieved to feel as if she belonged in this crowd, in a way she hadn't always felt like she belonged in her son's. His mind worked so differently to hers. She couldn't understand why they couldn't enjoy the simpler things in life together, why he couldn't be content with long summer days and company by the river. He seemed to occupy a world by himself and only a few people were allowed in. He would probably cause no end of problems with the social worker. Leah shuddered, praying that he didn't mention they had a social worker or their new address to her old friends.

'Elijah, why don't you and Reem go and sit under the tree there by the shade? I don't want you getting too hot in the sun.'

Leah caught up with her old friends; some threw questions in about the house but so far she avoided the topic. Her self-assured voice replaced the one she had become used to speaking in at home. She squashed the feelings of inadequacy and self-doubt and even managed to brush away any insecurity she had about being so recently widowed. That part was easy though, as they had barely asked about him. Beginning to feel that she could successfully play out the afternoon in her favour, Leah called Reem and Elijah over.

She instantly regretted it as Reem walked over. Her kimono was now wet around the edges from when she had helped Elijah, her cheeks looked slightly swollen and red under the midday sun, and she still hadn't removed the scarf that covered her hair. Leah felt hot just looking at her wrapped up in layers of material, while those around her wore shorts, T-shirts and straw hats. Elijah came over, his knees and hands muddied up from his incessant digging at the damp banks.

'Look at the state of you,' Leah said, rubbing the caked mud off his smart shorts as the faint smell of dried crustaceans wafted from his clothes.

'You look like a chimney sweep,' laughed Ed.

Leah had gone to school with Ed, the most outspoken one of the group. He was gangly and well-fed at the same time. Despite being the class clown, he always seemed to achieve high grades and graduate top of his class.

'And who is this? Did you hire a nanny, Leah?'

Leah stood back, realising her back was to Reem. 'This is Reem.'

'Your nanny?'

'No, my friend.'

'Where would you two have met? She doesn't appear to be a member of mummy and daddy's bridge club.' Ed laughed again, his footing unstable on the banks. His tall, thin physique always made him look off balance, like his feet didn't plant him firmly enough on the ground.

'Hey George, come and meet Leah's new friend,' Ed said, turning to speak to Leah, 'is she the reason we haven't seen you in a while?'

Leah looked on as they spoke to her. A few of their wives came over, too intrigued to stay in the shade of the bankside tavern. The questions they fired at Reem went unanswered, as Leah watched her look down vacantly, scuffing the sand with her foot as if they would stop talking if she just ignored them.

'Where's Emily?' Leah said, trying to change the subject.

'She told us she had invited you. She said she was shocked to see you the other day. Found it most unusual.' Ed paused, stirring the ice in his pitcher jug.

Leah placed her hand over her eyes as though she was searching for the boats in the distance.

George turned to Reem. 'Where are you from? How do you know Leah?'

Leah watched as Reem smiled nervously, glancing over at her to rescue her from the situation. Leah became increasingly nervous that something else might slip out. Her new life might be exposed. Had Emily told them about their agreement?

The boats began the race down their stretch of river, sending everyone's attention to the boats as cheers erupted on the banks and from the pubs alongside the shore. Leah took her chance.

'Come on, Reem, Elijah, let's paddle in the water. It is ever so hot and I think a dip might be exactly what we all need.'

Leah knew Reem wouldn't need any excuse to escape from the pack that had surrounded her. Elijah bounded up to them, happy he had company back. Leah kept opening her mouth, wanting to apologise, although she wasn't entirely sure why she needed to. Her mouth gaped like a fish as she tried to work out what to say. She hadn't noticed that Reem had stopped by the water. Her skin had turned damp and pale. Within seconds, she had dropped from her side into the soft mud with a thud.

Moments later, the people that had been spread out on the banks were all circling Reem. The boats had passed and now there was something else to watch.

'Oh no, Reem. What is it? Reem?' Leah stammered, kneeling down in the wet sand and loosening the clothes around Reem's neck. 'Stand back everyone, move out the way! Give her some air,' Leah said, kneeling down, her fingers shaking on Reem's weak pulse. 'Stop just staring, will you? Call an ambulance.'

There was an ambulance close by due to the crowds of people watching the race, so the paramedics arrived within a few minutes.

'I don't know what happened, maybe it's the heat. One minute we were standing there and the next she was down,' Leah told the paramedics, 'I haven't known her long, I mean, maybe she didn't drink enough water or something –'

'Can you hear me? What is your name?'

Leah watched helplessly as Reem remained motionless on the ground, her clothes becoming wet from the muddy water rolling in from the Thames.

The paramedics moved Leah to the side and counted to three as they went to lift her onto the stretcher. The ambulance was by the road, higher up the banks.

Leah and Elijah followed, leaving the crowds back on the beach. They had started to split off and get back to their afternoon, most of them piling into the tavern to watch the rest of the race on the TV.

'How many months is she?' they asked, when Reem was safely inside.

'Excuse me?' Leah wasn't paying attention as Elijah's hand could barely hold hers. It was clammy with sweat.

'Mummy, is Reem going to die?'

'No, darling, she just fainted. She will be fine.'

'When is her baby due?' the paramedic repeated again, wiping the sweat off his brow and making sure Reem was ready to go.

'What? What baby? She's pregnant?'

The paramedic looked at her but didn't say anything, so Leah continued, 'We don't know each other that well... She didn't tell me. Are you sure?'

The paramedic helped Elijah in. Leah sat opposite him, dumbfounded by what he had said, and looking at the firm roundness of her belly, now clearly visible through the thin kimono that had become tight around her middle as they lifted her. She hadn't noticed she was pregnant. How had she not noticed? Why had Reem not told her?

Leah sat silently in the back of the ambulance, staring at the strangers she shared the space with. Elijah's hand had slipped into Reem's.

~ *Reem* ~

She didn't recognise her surroundings when she came round. A familiar smell lingered in the air. A blanket was wrapped too tightly around her body. The lights were too bright and the monotonous beeping of the machine knocked into her mind. She shot up and ripped the drip from her hand, throwing her legs down onto the floor, almost falling as she tried to get out of the bed. The commotion made Leah wake up in the chair next to her. Elijah had fallen asleep on her lap.

'What are you doing to me? Why am I here?'

'You fainted at the river,' Leah said quietly, moving Elijah onto the chair.

Reem looked at her suspiciously. She felt her body in the hospital gown. The baby was there. There were no cuts. She looked at Leah. Leah looked confused. Reem sat back down, allowing the scenario to unfold around her. She was safe. She was on dry land. Leah knew about her baby.

'Why didn't you tell me?' Leah said, almost on cue, gesturing down to her stomach.

Reem shuffled back into a sitting position on the bed as Leah came over and checked the machines, looking at the drip in her hand.

'I thought maybe if I ignored it, it would go away.'

'Why would you think that?'

'Since I arrived, my thoughts... I don't know what's real anymore.'

'You can do this by yourself, Reem. You will probably feel different when the baby is here.'

'You don't understand. It isn't the same for me.'

'Well the baby is coming, Reem, so you need to try and prepare yourself. If you'd told me, I could've helped.

I wouldn't have dragged you around today for a start.' Leah had moved to the end of the bed and was now flicking through Reem's notes. 'You're both okay, you just fainted. It was probably the heat. Did you drink enough water –'

'I want to go home and have everything be like it was before.'

'Reem, I don't think it's that easy. Try not to get worked up, especially being pregnant – just take it one step at a time.'

But Reem was fixated on the thought of returning to what she had left behind. She was still convinced that it would happen; that she would return to her family home and they would pick up where they left off as though nothing had happened. She repeated it to herself in her mind, as though the repetition would make it a reality. She would find a way. But deep down, with the movements of her baby inside her, she knew that everything was going to change and she had no idea how she was going to make it work.

'Ah, Miss Ahmad,' the doctor said, opening the ward curtains and picking up the notes at the end of her bed. He glanced down at Leah.

'And Ophelia Streatfield. If it isn't my favourite student doctor.'

'Hello, Doctor Sameer. How are you?'

'Very well, you know how it is. Understaffed, over-worked,' he said, peering up at Reem as she sat upright in the bed. 'Have you decided to come back yet?'

'No, doctor. I decided it isn't for me.'

Reem looked at her, surprised. Whenever Leah snapped into work mode, when she was reading the notes or taking measurements from the machines, she imagined her working there effortlessly. She didn't believe that Leah didn't know that either.

'It seems your friend disagrees.'

Reem knew her face could never hide secrets well.

'How are you feeling now?'

'*Alhamdulilah*, doctor. Better. A bit faint still.'

'It's probably best we keep you in overnight just in case.'

'No, please doctor, I can't stay here.' She bolted up. 'I am actually fine. Really good,' she said, wincing as she tried to get down.

'Really?'

'Why don't you want to stay, Reem?' Leah asked, walking over and helping her up.

'Please, I don't like the hospital. Don't leave me here, Leah, please.'

Elijah woke up and stretched. 'Reem, you're okay!' he said, running over with such force that she toppled backwards when he hugged her.

'Be careful, Elijah. She's pregnant.'

'I know, mummy, I know.'

'I'll keep an eye on her, Doctor Sameer. I only live a few doors away.'

'Well, it's up to the patient. But if you do feel worse or your movements slow down from your baby, then you have to come back to emergency.'

'I will, I will,' Reem agreed willingly, as long as she didn't have to spend the night there.

'Oh yes, and before you leave, there is one more thing.'

Reem would have swallowed hard if she had any more fluids left in her mouth, but it tasted dry. Instead, she licked her lips.

'There were no records of your pregnancy on file.'

'No, I didn't tell anyone.'

'So this is your first medical check-up since you found out?'

Reem nodded. 'Is that a problem?'

'Yes, it is. But you already have a social worker, so I will inform her.'

Leah explained that because she had not seen a doctor or told anyone she was pregnant, she had not, according to the government, taken the necessary steps to ensure her baby was safe. Reem was in shock. She had hidden her baby, but she didn't want her to be sick.

'I didn't know if they would treat me and I don't have any money. I wouldn't want her unhealthy,' said Reem.

'I don't doubt that, Reem. But the doctors don't know you.'

'Will they take my baby?'

'I don't think so.'

'What if I don't understand what they want from me. I didn't know this before. I don't understand...' Reem's voice trailed off. She tried to sit up, straightening her back so she looked in control, but the flush of red through her cheeks and the stuttering of her words told everyone in the room that she wasn't.

'Don't worry,' said Leah, 'I'm not going anywhere.' Leah pulled Elijah close to her. 'We aren't going anywhere.'

Reem saw Elijah's smile light up his face. She looked at Leah, her forehead creasing slightly from the concern in her face, her hand spread out, palm upwards on the bed. Reem placed her hand in hers. *Alhamdulilah*, she thought. At least I'm not alone.

***

Reem had let her guard down, so much so that when someone knocked on the door, she ran over and opened it wide, expecting it to be Elijah. She was surprised to find she had unwillingly invited Jane in.

'I have come to see how you are after your hospital visit,' Jane said, bending down and slipping off her shoes at the door. 'Have you met your midwife yet?'

Reem sat down. 'No, but the doctor at the hospital checked.'

'Yes, they referred you. They're concerned that you haven't had any check-ups.'

'I'm fine.'

'And the baby?'

'The baby is moving.'

'That's very well; however, you still need to see a midwife to have checks every couple of weeks at least,' Jane said, wandering around the apartment.

Reem wasn't giving her full attention because in her haste to open the door, she had left her artefacts out on the table. Others were dotted around on the kitchen worktop waiting to be cleaned.

'These are beautiful,' Jane said, holding up a pearl-encrusted wooden box she had taken from the museum before it was bombed. It was over two hundred years old. 'Where did you get this?'

Reem walked over, trying to compose herself and look at the box as though it wasn't a priceless stolen relic.

'I think, this one is... my mother's,' Reem said, her hands shaking as she placed it back on the side.

'And this?' Jane said, sliding ancient coins between her fingers.

Reem took them from her hand and held them up against the light as if she needed to see them again to know that they were found buried under one of the old palaces. Worth a small fortune. But Reem hadn't stolen them for the monetary value, she reminded herself. She volunteered at the museum when it had happened. It wasn't like she went in that day, intending to steal.

'Just some of my father's old coin collection. Worthless, really,' she said breathlessly.

Reem wondered if Jane had seen straight through her lie. Wondering if the next knock on the door would be the police coming to arrest her, she blurted out, 'I haven't done anything wrong.'

Jane put them down and said, 'I am not here to judge you, Reem. All we care about is the health of you and your baby.'

Reem sat down, exhausted. She tucked the last few pieces under her throw on the sofa and prayed that Jane wouldn't find them.

'I don't know what will happen, as I am by myself.'

'As long as you're taking care of your baby, Reem, nothing happens. I'm here to help you both.'

Reem took a deep breath. If she did get arrested, she would never be able to find Adar. And what would happen to her baby?

Jane was able to stay longer than usual as her next visit was in the same building. Reem wasn't exactly happy about her prolonged stay but when the conversation changed to lighter matters, Reem felt like she might actually be getting somewhere. She told Jane how she planned to take English classes at the community centre and she was busy applying for jobs. Just short-term vacancies, as she wasn't sure how it would work when the baby arrived. Reem also told her that she was due to call the local area midwife that week. Jane seemed pleased with her progress and seemed to write less down this time. She left shortly afterwards, promising to return in a couple of weeks.

Reem closed the door behind her and quickly hid all of her museum pieces in a gap in the corner of the kitchen cupboards. But with them hidden from view, Reem felt lost. She took out one of the coins, wrapped it up in an old sheet of newspaper, and buried it into her pocket.

Chapter 6

~ *Reem* ~

The English classes at the community centre were held in the afternoon. The centre was only five minutes' walk away and Reem was keen to cram in as much as possible while she still had the time. She was shy about her English. Whenever she called agencies even for basic jobs, it was the first thing they asked. With no job, money was tight, and if she could get work then she would at least be able to eat better and buy the baby some clothes and blankets. Leah had kindly brought over a pile of stuff after she'd been discharged from the hospital, but she would need other things, and London was expensive. Even if she worked for a few weeks it would be worth it, and when the baby came, Reem was sure she could arrange some childcare.

'Reem, isn't it?'

Reem looked up and noticed one of the sisters from the gardening club.

'Yes, it is. Are you here for the English class?' Brianna said, juggling her bag which was overflowing with books and papers. She didn't wait for an answer. 'Come inside. I'm a bit late.'

Reem followed Brianna. Just inside the doors was an open area. In the corner, Reem saw prayer mats and copies of the Qur'an. Around the sides were tables and chairs stacked up. A few chairs had been pulled into the middle of the room and were occupied by another six women who turned to smile at her. Reem watched as Brianna dragged a whiteboard over to the centre of the room.

'Sorry I'm late, class. Is everyone ready to start?' Brianna said, signalling to Reem to sit down on the empty chair and desk.

'*Salam*, I'm Laila,' said a young girl next to her. Reem replied to her familiar accent and looked at the golden hair falling around her shoulders. She wore jeans and a tunic top and couldn't have been older than twenty.

'Where are you from?' Reem asked, because she dressed like she was from the UK, but her Arabic accent seemed closer to home.

'Palestine, then Syria, then here, I guess!'

Reem nodded, intrigued that she could fit in so well. She felt as if she stuck out wherever she went.

'How long have you been here?'

'A few years now,' Laila said, looking back toward the front of the room as Brianna begun.

'Right, so as you ladies can see, we have a new member today.'

Reem smiled weakly. 'I'm Reem.'

She was met with a chorus of welcomes. The women waved from their chairs and some even came over and shook her hand. Laila, she had already met. She couldn't remember the names of them all, or all the countries they had come from. She heard Malaysia mentioned as well as Sudan, the West Indies and Egypt... but they had no time to talk because after the quick intro, Brianna began.

Reem scribbled in her notebook as fast as she could, trying to keep up. It was clear that the class had been running for a couple of weeks already and the other students seemed to be writing down more than she was. The hour sped by and just as they were wrapping up, Chantelle burst through the doors.

'Hey everyone, don't mind me!' she said, waltzing over with a pile of printouts for her sister.

'Thanks,' Brianna said, then she turned to the class. 'Chantelle has made it just in time to drop off your extra study work. I have to go so see yourselves out, ladies, and I will see you all soon.'

The other women left when she did, picking up a pile of the work and dragging their chairs back to the side of the room.

'You don't cover?' Reem said, pointing to Laila's absent headscarf.

'I did, well, I do... I just don't like it sometimes.' Laila ran her fingers down her hair, pushing it back and twisting it behind her neck, almost hiding it. 'You know, standing out. It scares me a bit being obviously Muslim, after Paris.' She scribbled shapes down on the cover of her workbook, carving the lead into the front page.

Reem felt her scarf. She nodded, but she didn't really understand what Laila meant.

Chantelle overheard. 'Sometimes you have to stand out to be seen, you know,' she said, with her hands on her hips. Her outfit, a canary yellow, certainly stood out.

'Not everyone can pull off your look, Chantelle,' Laila said.

'I'm not talking about my clothes, girl. I was picked on at school. There weren't many dark-skinned girls in the school I went to when I was young, so I stood out.'

'I know how that feels,' Laila said.

'First I changed, you know, started dressing the same as them, tryna do my hair the same... well, that never worked, so after that I thought forget it. You gotta be who you are, you know.'

Reem hadn't thought about standing out until the day down at the river.

'Anyway, ladies, can't stand here chatting all day...'

When Chantelle left, Laila started moving the chairs and desks back to the sides of the room. Reem helped.

'Are you staying for *Asr* prayer?' Laila asked.

'Yes, of course,' Reem said, knowing that she had only the blank walls of the apartment to look forward to and had no reason to rush back.

After the prayers, Reem sat on the floor with Laila, talking about their shared memories of home. They spoke in Arabic, their mother tongue transporting them back to their homeland. Together, they left the grey concrete city and sailed across oceans to a time before the war, to bustling streets where purple hibiscuses and blooming jasmine flowers clambered over the city, infusing it with its sweet, perfumed scent. Together they scaled Jebal Kasioun to see over the city of Damascus, before drinking tea in Al Azem palace and watching the sun sink down into the Barada river.

Laila told Reem about how Palestine's old cities were similar to Syria's and since she had moved when she was young, the landscapes had morphed into one, so she couldn't distinguish the difference between the two. But this hadn't happened in London. It was too different to home. Flowers didn't fragrance the night-time air. The views over the city were from buildings, not mountains. The sun sank into puddles on the ground. A ground that didn't shake as jets raced through the skies. It had given her safety and she brought with it what she could. Laila pointed to the jasmine flower bracelet wound round her wrist, noticing the time on her watch as she did so.

'Oh no, I have to go. I'm late for work.'

'Where do you work?'

'Not far. You know that Turkish restaurant?' Laila said, taking off the prayer shawl and stuffing it back near the prayer mats.

'No, I don't.'

'Well, I work there at the moment,' she slipped off the prayer skirt and darted out the door. 'I will catch up with you here next time, *in'shaa'Allah*.'

'*In'shaa'Allah*,' said Reem.

Reem wandered around, skimming through some leaflets at the side of the room. They had places to go in London, free classes and courses and services that helped refugees and migrants. She took the ones that interested her and on the way out, she noticed Laila's bag on the floor. She picked it up, a phone poking out of the top. She had a rough idea of where Laila worked, and how many Turkish restaurants could there be?

She put the bag over her shoulder and headed out the door. She imagined Laila working front of house, waitressing with the big circular brass trays, covered with specially prepared mezzes. She probably wore a traditional Turkish gown in rich colours, with gold shining through underneath as she swished through the restaurant.

The restaurants Reem found along the street weren't the same as the upmarket restaurants back home. They were smaller – the size of cafes – and hectic, and there was certainly no Turkish dress. The staff wore black and white and the tables were close together. No tablecloths, just the mottled glass and metal chairs with cushion pads that were ripped from the seats. Shisha was being smoked outside where a few men gathered. They looked like regular shisha smokers with their brown-stained teeth and clothes that smelt of the damp plastic they were sitting under, as the sweet-smelling tobacco smoke puffed into the air.

'Hi, table for one is it?' a ruffled waiter said. His name badge read "Hakim".

'No, I was wondering if Laila works here?'

'She's round the back,' he said, leaving Reem to it and collecting dirty plates and glasses on his way back to the kitchen.

Reem wandered around the old men puffing away, avoiding the billows of white, apple-smelling smoke and dirty water dripping from the once-clear plastic that sheltered them.

She walked around the back where a narrow alley led to a back door. Reem walked down until she saw golden hair wrapped in a hairnet. She couldn't be sure it was Laila though, as she had her back to her and was at the back wall standing by the sink. Stacks of dirty dishes were piled on one side of two metal sinks. The water steamed up and the plates bashed against cutlery as they were dropped into the water. The waiters brought more in, and the pile never seemed to reduce. Once they were washed and rinsed, they were loaded into a dishwasher, the heat and smell of chemical lemons steaming up the kitchen. Reem tried to call her, but with the racket of the kitchen she knew she would have to wait. The waiter spotted her outside and went over to the girl and tapped her shoulder. She turned around and wiped her sweaty face with the top of her sleeve, as water ran down her blue washing up gloves. It was Laila.

She shouted to the cook that she was taking her break and struggled to get off her gloves and stop the taps, soaking herself with the grimy dishwater. She took off her hair-net and tried to smooth down her hair, frizzing at the edges from the humidity of the kitchen.

'Reem, what are you doing here?'

'Here, you forgot your bag.'

Laila looked down at it. 'Ah, stupid me! Thank you, *habibte*.'

'So this is where you work?'

'Yes, not exactly glamorous, but the boss is good. He doesn't want to see my papers or anything. I work, he pays me cash. It's easy.'

'You can't get settlement yet?'

'No, not yet. I'm waiting still and it was just too hard to live on nothing. I prefer to work...'

'Laila!' a voice shouted from the kitchen.

'I have to go. But thank you for this,' Laila said, hugging her handbag and jogging back into the kitchen.

'Yes, don't worry. You get back. I just wanted to drop it off for you,' Reem said, but she wasn't sure Laila heard.

***

Reem pulled out her London map to try and find the hotel where her job interview was. She had the papers showing she could work and realised that maybe not everyone had been so lucky. The street was busy and crowded. Tourists stopped in the middle of pavements to take photographs of phone boxes, open-top buses and famous street signs. Reem was staring at her map, trying to navigate which way to go and tripped on something, forcing her to stop and regain her balance. She glanced down to where she tripped and saw a grubby foot sticking out of a pile of rubbish. She followed the sleeping bag until she saw a head of red, tangled hair poking out of the top. A makeshift sign was stuck up next to a paper cup. She rummaged in her pockets and found the last bit of change she had and dropped it into the cup. Just a couple of metres from the homeless man stood the entrance to the hotel.

The hotel lobby doors were held wide open by the concierge: a short, plump man with red cheeks, exacerbated by his pillar-box red jacket trimmed with navy edging. The door closed softly behind her and shut out the noises of the street. Inside, it was like a different world. The plush, red carpet sank beneath her feet, the interior hallway and lobby was lit by rows of extravagant crystal chandeliers and the newly upholstered silver and crimson furniture shimmered under modern, diamond cut lights. Reem walked over to the mahogany reception desk and noticed it was inlaid with mother of pearl. It reminded her of Mahmoud's father, Abdullah. He had made that kind of furniture. Every piece of furniture in their house was beautifully handmade by him in their gardens and had paid for Mahmoud to attend the same private school as Reem. Sometimes she and Mahmoud would go into his work shed, where boxes of shells were piled near the work bench, ready to be polished and cut. The workshop was filled with the dust of shells and the aroma of glue and freshly carved wood.

During the evenings, she and Mahmoud would often return back from the *souk* to find Abdullah's workshop lit up discreetly. Out the back on its wide verandas, the men and women gathered under the hope of the stars to discuss the future of the country. Mahmoud would listen attentively from behind the trees and Reem would tell him how she imagined her future. He was always in it. Sat together, dreaming of what they could become.

He had dropped out of school that summer. He had become withdrawn since his father's workshop was burnt to the ground. It wasn't long after that Reem saw his carefree attitude beginning to extinguish. He had told Reem that he refused to join the army when his conscription was due, which was to be the year after he graduated from university. He shared his plan with her on how he was going to leave the country, and where he would go to start a new life. The last time she heard from Mahmoud was shortly after his father disappeared. He had become one of the missing. No one foresaw how quickly fortunes and lives can run out when war comes.

Reem ran her fingers over the edge of the reception desk, imagining how long this piece must have taken, thinking about its origin. It looked at least sixty years old by her estimation, but the design wasn't one she had seen before.

'Excuse me, can I help you?'

'Oh sorry, yes, hello,' Reem said, pulling her clothes loosely over her bump, cleverly concealed with an A-line floaty top she had found to wear under one of Leah's smart suit jackets.

'I'm here for the interview,' Reem said to the immaculately presented receptionist. The receptionist peered down through her turquoise-framed glasses, her eyes the same colour underneath, and smoothed down her blonde hair before leaning forward and whispering, 'Back house staff are not allowed to use the customer entrance.'

Reem looked down at the floor, noticing her cheap rubber shoes. She had once belonged in first class hotels, lunching with her parents, being known where she lived because of their longstanding status in the community.

'Excuse me, are you listening?'

But Reem wasn't listening. She was imagining the old days when the receptionist would have known who she was and piled her hands full of sweets and let her run around the lobby.

'Hello?'

'Sorry, what did you say?'

'I said, back office staff aren't allowed to come through this way.'

'Oh, okay. I will remember for next time.'

The receptionist looked down at her and Reem thought her expression seemed to say, 'If there is a next time'.

'What is your name?'

'Reem Ahmad.' Her Arabic accent pronounced the letters clearly. 'See Sylvia in Housekeeping.' Her English faltered, making her feel out of depth, which seemed to happen more often when she was nervous. She remembered what Leah had told her about her pronunciation and she took a deep breath, mouthing the sentence silently using her tongue and mouth to sound out the letters. The receptionist was looking at her strangely but had given up giving her any more lectures and sauntered off to the side door.

'If you go through this door to my right, turn left at the bottom and sign in at the security desk, then you will see the Housekeeping office to your right.'

Reem glanced at the door. A keypad locked it from the outside. She kept repeating the instructions in her head, but they were already a little blurry since she had said them so quickly.

Reem thanked her as she tapped in the code and opened the door. She stepped through and heard the door click. Inside, the decadent interior disappeared and was replaced by pared back walls painted in cheap magnolia paint, lined with luminescent strips, fire exit signs and artificial lighting. The white stripes on the floor guided her past noticeboards where she saw staff wearing different uniforms, pushing trolleys heaped with laundry that were almost as tall as themselves. She had completely forgotten where the receptionist had told her to go. She took what she thought was the first left, but there was no security station there. She kept walking until she reached the clanging pots and steaming heat of the kitchen. She retreated quickly back into the long corridors that seemed to stretch underneath the hotel, where its inner workings worked furiously below to create the serene atmosphere above. She became worried she would miss her appointment. She looked at her watch to check the time. It hadn't been there for months. It was still a habit of hers to imagine it was still on her wrist, the weight of it pressing down into her skin, the soft click of the dial as it turned.

'Can I help you?' a young voice said.

'Yes. Interview. With Housekeeping.'

'Come with me.'

Reem followed the young woman, who told her that her name was Kesandu. She followed Kesandu down the hallway, listening as she chatted about how long she had worked there, where she had come from, where she was going. Reem couldn't catch all of it and felt breathless when they arrived past the security desk, to a closed door with the sign 'Housekeeping' nailed to it.

'There you go.'

'Thank you.'

'Don't mention it,' Kesandu said. Just as she turned on her heels to leave, she jogged back up to Reem and said quietly, 'Sylvia likes you to say you want her job one day, even if you don't. Just a little tip for you.'

Reem didn't have time to reply because at that moment, the door opened and she was called inside.

Behind the desk, a strikingly tall woman sat typing away on her laptop. Her neat, blonde hair was scraped back into a tight knot at the back of her head. She closed the computer screen and carefully folded back her sleeves.

'You must be Reem.'

'Nice to meet you, Sylvia.'

'Professional, I like that. Are you here for front of house or housekeeping?'

Reem shrugged her shoulders. 'I don't mind.'

'How is your English?'

'I learnt English at school. But I'm taking classes too.'

'Great, we'll try you out and see what fits best.'

'Okay, thank you.'

'This is a very exclusive establishment though, Reem. You do understand the privilege of you working here?'

Reem didn't really know what to say, or understand what her point was. She remembered Kesandu. 'I would like your job.'

Sylvia's back straightened. 'Excuse me?'

'One day, I would like to be in your job.'

Sylvia's body softened back into the curve of her chair.

'Yes, I can see why. When can you start?'

On her way out, after all formalities had been agreed, Reem looked for Kesandu to thank her but she couldn't see her anywhere. She mustn't forget to thank her, she thought.

Reem strutted through the lobby and felt her feet sink into the carpet. Maybe things were starting to look up. The sun shone in the bright blue sky, but there was a cool breeze that felt fresh against her cheeks. Instead of going back on the underground, Reem wanted to feel more of the sun on her face. After all, this was a turning point. She was becoming part of a life she had only seen on films.

***

It wasn't as if she had meant to go into that particular building. She had stumbled upon it as it sat within the modern city. It must have taken decades to build. Each pane of glass, the details in the brickwork, the carved statues outside and the sweeping ramps that led to its grand entrance, like an open mouth, beckoned her inside.

If she had known it was the Natural History Museum, she probably wouldn't have gone inside. If she knew that it was a place for the preservation of all dead things, she would have stayed outside beneath the open span of the sky.

Instead, she stood underneath the skeleton of a blue whale. The size of its bones pulled across the ceiling. The unusual way they formed the beak of its mouth, had turned this gentle, majestic creature into an alien, otherworldly. It made her feel insignificant. There was something unnerving about it. The creature who had swallowed Yunus. Then, as commanded by his Lord, the whale had thrown Yunus out onto a beach. The skeleton of the great creature was now strung up, suspended. Its empty innards proudly displayed in a grand, old building in the middle of a city, miles away from the sea.

Reem didn't realise how long she had been staring up at it until she was brought back down by the sound of her home language; something that she didn't hear all the time. It rang out like a familiar chime in the air. She turned around to see a group of young children being escorted by their teachers. Something about their confidence in their

Arabic dress, their black gowns that fell loosely to the floor and the sash of the charity-assisted primary school around their shoulders as they switched effortlessly between Arabic and English, intrigued Reem enough to walk over.

'*Salam alaikom*,' Reem said, the words flowing naturally out of her mouth.

'*Wa alaikom salam*,' the teacher in the sepia-coloured *abaya* stood closest to her, replied.

'I am from Syria. You?'

'Hackney,' was the teacher's reply.

Reem stood there as she watched the teacher huddling the children through the crowds of people. She was sure they would be able to talk to her, to respond in Arabic, but even though she looked like she could belong here, she realised she didn't. She reached into her pocket and felt the uneven, bumpy gold coin. She daydreamed about her old town. She felt the warmth of the sun on her back and the familiar sounds of the athan in the air. She sometimes thought she heard it in the skies over London, but she would have been mistaken.

Reem found herself standing by a tank filled with an ageing liquid she thought she had smelt before. Inside was a marlin, its eyes intact, its scaly skin barely keeping together around its body, and its long snout drooping slightly from decay. The way it stood motionless, encased like a child in a womb, not realising, made her feel sick. She placed her hand to her stomach and rushed down the hallway adjacent to the main hall. She was surrounded by lifelike animals, positioned with mouths open, teeth bared. She looked closely at the rough fur, the eyes made of glass. She pressed against the windows into the cabinets. The fur was real. The tough prickles of hair stood on edge, slight bald patches appeared where the dead skin had been stretched over a mould – or could it have been its actual carcass? Reem had never seen anything like it. They weren't fake. These were dead animals, gutted, dried out and stuffed. The sun beat down through the conservatory roof and made her head spin. She hurried through, slipping in between the families and tourists posing for photographs near the glass.

Sharp instruments, laid out skins, pieces of bones. She lurched over in the nearest bin and threw up. The rocking motion had returned to her legs. Adar. The boat. The heaving dark waves beneath. She weaved through the exhibits until she reached the fresh air outside. She centred herself on the steps and pressed her hands over her skin. She thought she felt the rough patches of scars underneath her clothes. She tore them up to see but there was nothing there. Only the scar she had had since she was a child when she had fallen from the pomegranate tree.

Down on the floor, a leaflet wedged itself under her foot. It was in Arabic. It was a sign.

***

Reem left the Tube station and turned right onto Edgware Road. She read the numbers on the shop and began the long walk down. As she did, London shifted around her. It became more familiar. She could read. Arabic writing was curved boldly on the signs, the smells from the shops wafted under her nose. She could smell things she was used to: cardamom, scented tobacco, the smell of frying falafel.

Eventually she reached number 172, the place that the flier had advertised. But next door, something had caught her eye as objects glinted from the windows. The doorbell rang as she walked in. Laid out in front of her were antiques from all over the globe that she had never seen before, encased in glass.

'Do you have something you want to sell?' said a voice sitting behind the counter.

Reem felt in her pocket. 'No, I was looking for something.'

'What?'

'It is a ring, a very distinctive ring, a trio of stones made of lapis lazuli,' Reem said in Arabic, scanning the items behind the glass. She recognised some Eastern pieces. Some of them she was certain were Syrian antiquities. The way they were made, the shapes of the stones. The curved angle on the spouts of the jugs. They were mostly Syrian.

He got up and walked over to the glass, breathing heavily on it.

'Nothing here that matches that description,' he said, after scouring the necklaces. 'Is there nothing you want to sell?'

Reem shook her head and gripped her coin tightly in her hands. She wasn't ready to let go.

By the time she left the shop it was almost dusk. A waiter was preparing tables outside under a canopy. The restaurants and cafes were beginning to fill up. A group of women walked past her, their familiar accents catching Reem off guard. She stood closely listening, closing her eyes, imagining that it was her mother and her aunty in the courtyard. How she wished now that she was tired from preparing food for the family, how she wished to be cooking Adar's favourite dish as he played around her feet. The loss of it caused her to lean against the wall. It made her feel dizzy. Her body felt out of balance.

'Eat with us, sister?'

Reem looked at the woman in front of her. She was around her mother's age and spoke with the accents she had heard from the capital back home.

Reem shook her head and tried to protest, embarrassed at how ill she must have looked leaning up against the wall. She wanted to tell the woman that it wasn't hunger that made her body weak. It wasn't water that she needed. It was for things to return to how they were. It was a home she was sick for, a life she had planned out, filled with those she loved. Mostly it was the loneliness of her existence, as she wandered to and fro aimlessly, looking for treasures to remind her of home.

Reem knew she had no choice but to sit. Once you are invited to join a family for dinner, all refusals are met with even more determination for you to be involved. Shortly afterwards, the waiter opened the door and brought out steaming plates of rice, chickpeas and sultanas with grilled whole fishes placed on top. Undressed salads were sprinkled with salt and lemon juice was squeezed on top. Other salads, finely chopped, were decorated with pomegranate seeds and sumac. The aromas of spices wafted under her nose; hints of cardamom, cumin and turmeric.

Once Reem had eaten and drunk, she felt calmer. Her veins were quenched and her body began to feel better. As the eating slowed down, the conversation increased. Reem answered questions about where she was from and what home was like. The women shared their stories of how they arrived in England, what they left behind and who they had lost. The stories made Reem feel part of something. She wasn't the only one. The loneliness evaporated and for the first time she listened attentively, happy to be immersed in the country she was desperately trying to cling on to.

'You've heard of them selling their organs. We have nothing left to give but to sell our body parts.'

Reem dropped her glass of tea. She shot up from her chair, her hands burning, the glass shattered by her feet. Iqra grabbed some napkins and shouted to the waiter for ice water.

'Are you okay?'

Reem nodded, but Iqra knew. She looked at her.

'It has affected you. How did you arrive?'

'I paid someone. On a boat.'

'I have heard these stories. Those people, they sell their soul to the devil.' Iqra spat dryly to her left side. 'Where do you live? Do you know anyone from home here?'

Reem told her mostly the truth, but suddenly the thought of home no longer comforted her. Their journeys here were fraught with risks. Her own memories buried under the piles of rubble and broken souvenirs in the apartment, her preoccupation to find her mother's ring, her failure to find her brother and to dig up the truth about her own survival, her own involvement, was too much.

'And you have to take care of yourself, and...' her voice trailed off as the waiter came over. She pulled at her top. The roundness from her full stomach felt as if it was more obvious. Reem placed her hand into her pockets to help pay the bill, even though she knew she had nothing in them.

'Let me help, I have something –'

'Don't insult me, dear! You were our guest.'

Reem automatically pulled out the coin and it fell from her hands. Iqra knelt down to pick it up.

'I recognise this. Where did you get it from?'

Reem felt an underlying tone of suspicion. She took it back a bit too eagerly from her hands.

'It belonged to someone I know.' She stuffed it back into her pocket like a thief stashing his loot. Hidden. Stolen. A payment for a life. Reem sensed Iqra could tell what she was hiding. Reem had let her guard down. She fell too easily into the comfort of it all. They had reminded her of back home before she had come here. Before she had lost Adar. She had relaxed too much. She was in danger of forgetting.

In the busyness of the street, she saw a young boy pass by her. From behind, he looked strikingly like Adar. Even his walk was the same. She called out his name but as he turned, she saw it wasn't his face. How could it be? This boy was with a family and she knew Adar was alone. She felt sick, her stomach tightening, almost as if it was going to disintegrate. Her mind snapped back to the marlin, floating but dead, preserved in chemicals, decaying at the seams, wanting to disintegrate. She wondered if people saw how hollow she was, the way her body felt like it didn't belong to her, in a country that wasn't hers. But the movements inside her reminded her that she was alive and what was coming was going to make it almost impossible to return home. A new life, in its own waters, growing inside her.

chapter 7

~ Reem ~

Reem was asked to cover the front of the hotel, to greet guests and serve drinks. She didn't want to protest as after all, she had only been there a few days and the usual staff member that was supposed to be there was off sick. She was shown into the closet that stocked the uniform and was asked to change. She chose an oversized blouse, kept her only pair of trousers on that fit, and tried to hide her bump by wearing one of the male aprons that came down to her knees. She hoped Sylvia wouldn't notice. She walked around the lobby, guiding guests to the drinks bar, feeling much more suited to a front of house position. This was where she spent most of her childhood. Her mother and father attended lunches and meetings in the hotels, discussing business and weddings and various celebrations. Mahmoud would usually be there with her and they would go off and sit on a table by the window by themselves, imagining that they were lunching alone. He would tell her that he was going to marry her and they could forge their own life together, anywhere she wanted to be. She glanced at the empty table and chairs by the window. She wondered if he was even alive now. How naïve they had been to daydream as they had.

It turned into a busy weekday morning, with most of the clients being businessmen and women who were checking in for a week of meetings in the city. People began streaming through the doors and asking questions. She directed most of them to the receptionist's desk and was relieved that she was handling it all today. Reem realised she didn't know London. She couldn't answer questions on the city, or the transport to get to certain places. Most of the clients wanted to check in and the least she could manage was to direct them to the customer service desk.

It was going without incident, until a middle-aged, prematurely balding man came in, dabbing his forehead with a white handkerchief. He asked Reem a question, but his accent was heavy. She hadn't heard it before. The words rolled off his tongue, impossible to decipher.

'Excuse me?'

'Don't make me repeat myself,' he said, and began to raise his voice.

Reem wasn't sure what to do.

'Please, go to the receptionist,' Reem stuttered, flustered under the volume of his voice, 'she can help you.'

'All you lot coming over and taking British jobs. I'm from Scotland. You know, part of the same island, but I guess you immigrants don't know that.'

He was making such a scene that Sylvia rushed over. Reem saw her glance in horror at the ensemble she had pieced together and then cut in between the two of them.

'I'm sorry, can I help you, sir?' Sylvia said in her placid, firm tone. She turned to Reem. 'Go and take a break in the back. I will talk to you shortly.'

Reem walked off into the back office that sat just inside the lobby, relieved to be in the cooler area, her cheeks burning, her mouth dry. Her English wasn't good enough.

She couldn't even look the part. She realised any similarity between her old life and this was gone. She was not seen here the same way she was back home. Here, she was an impostor. Reem paced the back office. Sylvia came in and shut the door behind her.

'Reem, you said you can speak English. That was not acceptable.'

'I can, but I didn't understand his accent. I am taking classes...'

'We're short-staffed so lucky for you, I can't let you go yet. And seeing as though you're only temporary...' Sylvia paused, looking her up and down. She spoke her next words slowly, 'Finish off helping Jonathan, then you can change and stay in the back, and we will see how you go from there.'

'But – I...'

'Is there another problem?'

Reem shook her head.

'Good. I'll have to make do with you until my proper front staff arrive. Just try to stay out of trouble, please.'

Reem went back out. The man had gone. She walked over to the bar and told Olek she was there to help until someone else began their shift shortly.

She half-hid behind the bar, her feet becoming swollen from standing.

'Leah? Is that you?' Reem said, walking over to a blonde-haired woman stood at the door. It was Leah, although she looked different. She wore a rose gold silk jacket over short ankle-length trousers and her neck was covered with a silk pashmina.

'Reem, what are you doing here?'

'I got the job. This is where I work.'

'Congratulations, that's great news! Come and join us,' Leah said, gesturing to the table where Leah's parents were already sitting down.

Reem walked over with her hand out, ready to greet them both.

Barbara dismissed it with a wave and proceeded to order. 'A bottle of Laurent Perrier Rosé Champagne, please.'

'Oh, I – Yes, sure, let me go and get that for you.'

'Mum, dad, this is my neighbour.'

'Bring some water with that too, Voss. None of that tap water with ice nonsense.'

'Mum, I've asked Reem to join us.'

'Friends with the staff now, are we?' Barbara said to Leah, her eyebrows raised to show her disapproval.

'She lives next door to me. Elijah and I have been spending time with Reem since we moved.'

'Jolly good. That's great that you have a good friend close by. Where are you from? You don't look like you're from around here.'

'I live in North Kensington,' Reem answered, still standing, unsure what to do about the drinks order.

'Sit down, we will call over one of the bar staff,' Phil said, clicking his fingers in the air. 'I know where you live, but where are you from?'

'Syria. I came here from Syria.'

'We have some lovely Syrian furniture. You lot are good at that handmade stuff. Remember, Barbara, the unit we have in the lounge?'

Barbara forced a smile.

'What do you think of good old England so far then?'

'It's different... but – I'

'Probably a good thing it is different, eh? Syria looks like a hellhole when I see it on the news. What a disaster.' Phil paused briefly to give the order to the waiter who had come over. 'What was I saying? Oh yes. Hellhole, that place.'

Reem fidgeted with the hem of her blouse. Her mind returned home. Even in the midst of war, she hadn't compared it to hell. She reminisced about the warm air, scented with apricots.

'That's why you're all coming over is it?' Barbara said.

'Well, erm. It is dangerous now. There aren't many safe places left. Like where we used to live, it –'

'I couldn't stand to live somewhere like that. It must be much better here. You're lucky you managed to get here.'

'Mum, have you ever considered that maybe she didn't want to leave?'

'Don't be silly, Leah. Who on earth would want to stay there rather than come here?'

'That's her home.'

'Look at your home now. I bet that's akin to living in a war zone.'

'Oh mum, stop being so dramatic.'

'Well, I'm just saying. It's practically like living in the Calais Jungle over there. That's probably why your friend likes it so much. And poor Elijah, he'll probably start speaking in another language soon if he goes to one of those schools,' Barbara said, contorting her face.

'Why would that be a bad thing?' Leah said, noticing her reaction.

'Come on, you two. Leave it for now. You're making what's-her-name feel uncomfortable,' Phil tried to intervene, but Leah interrupted.

'Her name's Reem.'

'I'm sorry, I don't know Arabic,' her mum said afterwards.

Reem didn't know where to look. She saw Leah roll her eyes and bury her head in her hands.

'I have to get back to work now,' Reem said, standing up from her chair and sliding it back neatly under the table.

'I don't blame you,' said Leah, firing a glare at her parents. 'We will catch up soon. I'm sure Elijah will be over to see you tomorrow, if you aren't working?'

Reem nodded and dashed off back towards the bar.

'You don't let her look after Elijah, do you?' her mum asked.

'Sometimes, yes. Why? What's the problem?'

'You have no idea who she is. She could be anybody. You can't trust them.'

'Who is "them", mum?'

Reem was relieved that she was too far away to hear Barbara's answer.

'Could you take over, please?' Reem said to Olek, who was polishing glasses behind the bar. Reem was beginning to feel faint. She hadn't felt like this before and couldn't place the feeling. She felt hollow and nauseous, like a pain was growing through her stomach to her heart.

'What's happened now?'

'I don't like being front of house. On display, people looking.'

'It isn't for everyone,' Olek said, taking delight in smoothing down his uniform and his fair, almost white-coloured hair, before strutting out to take their order.

'Hi, I'm sorry I'm late. I'm Claire. You've been covering for me.'

Reem looked at her as she stood behind the bar and slipped off her trainers for expensive heeled shoes, and tied her straw-coloured hair in a sleek ponytail at the back of her head.

'I was late because there were engineering works on the train line, always happens on my route,' she laughed, tucking spare clothes into a bag and wiping the heavy make-up off her face.

'There she is, at last. Let me guess. Traffic?' She and Olek laughed at the shared joke. Claire straightened her jacket and tossed her oversized bag under the counter. She picked up a glass tray of drinks at the side of the bar, looked at Olek, and glided out onto the floor to serve them.

Reem slipped through the staff entrance back door, looking around at the cream corridors, sparse walls and cheap lighting. She peered back through the window to the drinks bar and saw how elegant Olek and Claire looked in the lobby. The customer areas were aglow with delicate lighting and the faint hum of serene music. Reem looked down at herself. She may have been part of a society like that before, but realised she wasn't anymore. She couldn't even manage to fit in doing basic work. The feeling that she didn't belong was a new one. Maybe Laila had a point about her headscarf. Maybe removing it would be one less barrier to her being accepted. But as she unwrapped it and looked at her reflection, she realised she knew herself even less without it.

~ Leah ~

Leah watched Reem disappear behind the bar. She felt a little relieved as she didn't want to be in the position of asking her parents for help and have Reem overhear.

89

'I don't think we need to point fingers. The social worker obviously visited because you aren't fit to give Elijah what he needs,' her mum said, perching on the end of her chair.

'Don't you dare, mum. I would die for him.'

'No one is disagreeing with that,' her dad said, placing his hand firmly on his wife's knee. 'All we are saying is, let us help you. Move back. We can help with his school fees.'

'That is what the social worker wanted, wasn't it? For him to go back to school?' Barbara said.

'Any school, mum.'

'Oh and you would have him at one of those inner city schools, would you? Poor boy would never have a chance to fulfil his potential. What he needs is his old school, his old classes and extra-curricular activities –'

'I haven't decided what's best for him yet,' Leah said, swallowing the water in her glass. She hoped it would quell the disappointment pumping through her. She desperately wanted her old life back, but instead it was fading away and being replaced by a different one. Leah felt guilty that in some ways the move had made her feel better. Although she had no choice but to give away Matthew's clothes and move away from their memories together, it had inadvertently helped her through the grieving process. She never intended to erase him out of her life, but she had begun to transition and she didn't know if that made her feel comforted or even more distressed. It felt as if everything was slipping through her hands and she couldn't keep hold of it.

'And your old house. It isn't out of the question that you could go back there.'

'Barbara, we said we wouldn't...'

'Oh, be quiet, Phillip. There's nothing wrong with offering our daughter help. But of course it would come with certain... certain criteria.'

'There you go again, mum, trying to control me and now Elijah.'

'Loving you and wanting the best for you both isn't controlling.'

'You don't know what's best for us. I don't even know yet.'

Leah realised how true that was. She had been sleeping better since she had moved and it wasn't just her. There was something different about Elijah too. He was making friends easier, he was relaxed, and he seemed to be enjoying his own free time. Maybe the change of environment did him good. She was also able to spend more time with him instead of ferrying him from one after-school class to another. He hadn't had nightmares since.

Phillip glanced at the clock, his knee shaking. 'Barbara, we have to go now. I have that meeting and I can't be late.'

'What meeting?'

'With the council, darling. Just a business meeting. We've won a contract and I'm busy outsourcing it. We have a few loose ends to tie up.'

'Is business picking up?' Leah asked.

Phillip looked at Barbara swilling the last of the champagne around her glass before gulping it down. She pressed her lips together tightly before saying, 'We are throwing a small soirée. You can even invite your friend, whatever her name was.'

Leah reluctantly agreed, thinking only of how much Elijah enjoyed visiting his grandparents' house and playing with all his old toys in their garden. She even thought briefly about the dinner. A three-course dinner, she thought, and her stomach began to groan.

'Fine, I'll come, but only for Elijah.'

Leah noticed her mum's mouth almost smirking, cracking the foundation around her lips.

'Before you leave, mum, you might want to thank the Alcotts down the road. They've offered me a cleaning job and I took it.'

Leah enjoyed watching the disgust on her mum's face.

'No, you haven't.'

'Yes, I have. So now I will be able to pay for things myself for the first time.'

'Let's see how far you get, shall we?' Barbara said, before throwing a bunch of notes on the table and marching out the door.

Phil stood up and kissed Leah on the forehead. 'I'm sorry, darling, you know your mother.'

Leah watched silently as they left the hotel. She looked at her watch. Her first cleaning shift was due to start within the hour. She winced at the thought. But with her savings running out and her bills due in the next few weeks, she refused to let her son go hungry. She scooped up the generous tip her mum left and headed out the door.

When Leah walked down her old street she couldn't help but stare at her old home. It looked the same as it had when she packed up their things and left. It looked as perfect now as it did then. Even more so since she knew she couldn't have it back.

Leah thought she wouldn't have minded as much if it wasn't for her memories of Matthew being there. She remembered how on long summer evenings, he cooked for them in their farmhouse oven and how afterwards he would dance with her in the garden. She daydreamed about how Elijah would fall asleep on his lap, swinging on the wicker chair that hung from the oak tree.

In the garden, she used to hear the gentle humming of bees from their beehive. Leah used to watch them perch on the flowers, collecting pollen, their bodies defying gravity as they buzzed to and from the beehive. If she could have taken those memories or other memories of him with her, then maybe she wouldn't ache to have the house back so intensely. Whenever she looked at it, she saw him there. Since she had left, she didn't want to admit that his face was erasing itself from her memory. It became distorted. Sometimes she saw it in Elijah but just when she tried to remember him, to feel the familiar contours of his jaw and his cheekbones, he morphed into a stranger. It would become a detached part of her. Like the bodies in medical school. A stiff dummy that didn't bleed, that could be taken apart and put back together; a machine with broken parts that she thought she could fix. But whenever it was cut open, operated on and stitched back together, it would never look the same. Like a ragdoll, sewn up.

She hadn't taken the bees. Since she had left, she had had nightmares about them being abandoned in the garden. Their humming changed into the sound of piercing drones, deafening. Swarming the garden, so many bees, she couldn't see through them. Elijah ran to meet her and they surrounded him. Stinging his face, his neck, his throat, as she watched helplessly on. Another person she couldn't fix.

The Alcotts lived on the same street so it was inevitable that she would pass by her old house. Leah went around to the back gate. It didn't look like anyone was in. She peered through the windows, but she couldn't see in because the nets were restricting her view. She couldn't even tell if it was lived in. The back gate was locked. She pressed her ear against the painted teal wood and listened. The garden was silent.

She walked the short distance to Emily's house and stood at the doorway, ringing the chiming bell that echoed through the house. No one answered so she unlocked it with the spare key Emily had given her. She knew she needed the money and the sheer satisfaction of seeing her mum's face had made it worthwhile, until the moment she walked in. The freestanding kitchen was larger than her and Reem's apartment put together. They must have had it recently refurbished because it had been opened out onto the garden and spanned the same distance as the lounge. Every surface of the kitchen was full of unwashed saucepans and plates from the night before. The lounge adjacent to it was covered with rubbish and dirty wine glasses, empty packets, dried up plates of food on serving plates and half-drunk bottles of wine littered the sides. They'd had a party the night before. She dreaded to think how many more rooms were sprawled out in this deceiving space. By the time she reached upstairs, she was exhausted. Luckily it wasn't as bad upstairs, so it was easier for her to dust and polish and make the beds. In one of the spare bedrooms she saw a long term care bed stripped bare – even the mattress was gone. Paint strips and wallpaper samples were strewn on top of it. An armchair sat by the window. Leah could see her building from there, almost framed in the view.

Leah finished by cleaning the glass bi-fold doors downstairs that opened into the garden onto a newly paved area. There, at the back of the house, was Emily's apiary. Emily owned the urban beekeeping company that had provided their own hive. She opened the back door to throw the rubbish out, and seeing the garden reminded her of her commitments that afternoon. She smiled. Was she looking forward to it even? She collected her money, which had been left downstairs in an envelope on the kitchen side and opened it up, counting the crisp notes inside. It was enough to feed them and there was some left over for bills for the week, but even if she worked until the end of the month, it would never be enough. She knew she would have to find more work after the summer but she also held onto the fact that her parents wouldn't see them struggle. They would give in eventually, she thought.

Leah was interrupted by the front door opening. Emily walked in wearing her dark sunglasses. It looked like she wearing make-up from the night before. Leah could tell by the look on her face that she had forgotten this was her cleaning day. Emily stood at the door looking at the house, then glanced at Leah in her cleaning clothes.

'Honey, I completely forgot it was today. What a disaster,' she said, throwing her lambskin handbag down onto the now clean worktop. 'You know my Ray, he drinks far too much and it always gets out of hand. On top of that, his father has been getting progressively worse.'

'I didn't know... I...'

'Yes, well, it was his house but Ray and I just couldn't take him living here anymore. Every day he would wander down the stairs, goodness knows where his mind was. He kept saying the people from the tower were watching him.'

'You mean the building on the green, near the Alif Community Centre?'

'How do you know it? Yes, look, you can see it from our window. An eyesore really, but you know, what are we supposed to do about it? At least it will be getting a facelift soon. It won't look so ghastly. Anyway, so Arnold just kept saying that it was watching him. Late stages of Alzheimer's, you know. He even said he lived there once but I don't see how. So we moved him to the Mews.'

'The old people's home?'

'Well, Ray doesn't like to call it that. He prefers "assisted living". And of course, it is expensive. Cost us a lot of money so Arnold had no choice really but to sign over the house. It isn't like it was in good condition. We did him a favour, really.' Emily only paused to pull out some aspirin from her bag. 'Pass me the water out of the fridge please, sweetie, I can't drink the tap water around here.'

Leah watched the tablet fizzing in the clear water, clouding it.

'Anyway, how rude am I being? How are you?' she said, taking off her sunglasses and pulling her lips into a downward smile.

Leah collected her keys and stuffed the envelope into her bag.

'Fine, just busy after the party last night,' she said, instantly regretting bringing it up.

'Well, you know it's funny, I did think of inviting you, but I just didn't think it was your scene now, you know after... so anyway, if I can do anything, you know I'm here for you. All you have to do is ask.'

'Would you have a look at doing an apiary on a residential building, like a building block?'

Emily looked surprised. 'Yes, well, I can get the boys to have a look. Why? Where have you moved to?'

'It would just be a favour, really. For Elijah.'

'Okay, let it be my gift to him. He really is such a cutie pie and Aaron misses him dearly at school. He's been through enough at his tender age and now not being with his friends, really, it breaks my heart.'

Leah couldn't answer. She just took the business card of one of Emily's beekeepers and left, closing the door behind her.

***

That evening she headed to the garden club for their weekly meeting. Mo had reminded her that the next meeting was to be held that afternoon. And perhaps because the invitation had come from him, Leah and Elijah found themselves back on the eighth floor waiting for the meeting to start, and Leah was hoping that no one would notice that she had actually arrived early. The now familiar faces began appearing and Leah felt more relaxed. When Mo entered, Leah went straight over to him.

'Hi Mo.'

'Hi Leah, are you okay?' he said, looking down at his feet.

Leah ignored it and carried on, excited by the news she had. 'I've arranged for someone to come and assess the building to see if we can keep a hive here.'

Mo looked up. 'Really? That would be great for the garden. We could grow more wild flowers, and maybe even look at jarring up our honey. It would be such an asset... but –'

'What is it?'

'We don't have any budget left.'

'It's okay, I know her. It won't cost us anything.'

'Wow, that's quite a gift. She must be a good friend.'

Leah half smiled, and it broke into a beam as she saw Elijah appear after watering the pots.

'Mummy,' he said, running over.

'How do you fancy being my chief beekeeper?' Leah said.

'Really? We can get another one? You promise?'

Leah laughed. 'Hold on there! Emily said she might be able to do it. But they have to come and check it's suitable here and –'

'And I can learn how to do it now that I'm nearly ten?'

'You know I don't like you close to the bees. Just in case.'

'Oh mum, I'll be fine. What do you think, Mo?'

'About the beehive?' Mo answered, as he swept up some compost that had fallen out of the bag.

'Yeah,' Elijah said, nodding excitedly.

'Sounds like a good idea to me, mate. But you're going to be a busy bee yourself.'

'How come?' said Leah.

'He's decided his next project will be a Middle Eastern garden.'

Leah raised her eyebrows and smiled at Elijah. He told her he wanted to do a Middle Eastern themed garden for Reem. She had told him about pomegranates and date palms, and he wanted to have a go in the empty corner where the potatoes had already been harvested for the summer. Chantelle said she could donate some pots for him to start with and Nidal gave him some date seeds, wrapped in his pocket.

Brianna laughed. 'And you were just going to throw those away! Look how happy they've made him,' she said, watching him dart off to find somewhere to put them.

No one had pomegranate seeds but Mo said he would keep an eye out and maybe if they could afford to go to the Turkish restaurant over Ramadan, he would pinch a few off the tops of the salads there.

The meeting started shortly afterwards and the subject of cladding came up again. There had been no response from the council and the builders were already in the stairwells, busy working on transforming the façade of the building.

'It does look better,' Chantelle said. 'It doesn't look so old.'

'We used it once, back when I was in the trade. When I threw my cig on it, it started smoulderin' straight away. It's like dressin' up a box. Only makes it look better, it don't do nothin' else,' Bill said.

'Looking better is a big thing, ya know,' Chantelle said, flicking her hair, now styled in a sleek long ponytail over her shoulder.

Brianna was sat next to her and briefly stopped writing notes when Chantelle's hair flicked her face.

'They aren't just doing the cladding though. They're upgrading other areas like the hallways,' Brianna said.

'Yeah, we don't want them to stop that. It desperately needs some TLC,' Chantelle said, agreeing with her sister.

'They ain't doing it right though,' Nidal said, coming forward from the edge of the group. 'None of us can afford to move out, right?'

The sisters nodded and Bill shrugged.

'So they know that. What's the average price of a house here?' Nidal said, looking over at Leah.

'Two, three million?' Leah said, knowing it was more than that if they were talking averages, but it already sounded too high.

'That's my point. We ain't got a choice but to stay. They want it to look like it's better, but it ain't helping how we live.'

'True. The lifts are still broken,' Chantelle said.

'And we still ain't got lighting outside past midnight and I know more than one of us works two jobs just to pay our rent.'

'So what we gonna do about it?' Chantelle said directly to Nidal. 'Do ya have a plan?'

'Let's just keep the pressure on and see what happens,' said Mo. 'We know they have it in their budget and I have to believe that they'll do the right thing.'

No one commented, but Leah read their faces and could tell they didn't necessarily agree with his optimism.

'Now onto something I think we'd all love. Leah, do you want to tell everyone?'

'We are going to arrange for someone to come and see if we can get a beehive here.'

There was a general cloud of noise, mostly positive, Leah thought.

'It isn't confirmed yet, but with bees endangered and hives popping up all over London, there shouldn't be any reason why we can't have our own. I'll keep you all posted.'

'Be good if we could sell our own honey,' Bill said.

'I don't know if it would make that much, would it, Leah?' said Brianna.

'I'm not sure yet but like everything, if we try it, we can find out. Ours used to make a few kilos a year, so not bad really.'

Chantelle and Brianna nodded in unison.

'Thank you, Leah, that would be a great achievement for us all here,' Mo said, looking over at her. Leah pretended not to notice and hoped the glow emanating from her cheeks was known only to her. 'And for those of you who were wondering what we were going to do with the empty area near the potatoes, our newest member Mr Elijah has had an impressive idea to see if we can have a Middle Eastern themed corner so we are handing that over to him.'

The gardeners clapped in unison.

'Now it's that time of year again and I could do with someone to help with the Big Iftar.'

Chantelle was filing her nails, Brianna was too busy studying for exams, and Bill muttered something about his lack of culinary skills.

'I will do it,' Leah said, surprising herself. 'Well, maybe not. I mean, I can't cook very well.'

'You don't have to cook, unless you want to?' Mo said, looking pleased that she had offered. 'You could just help gather people together, make sure they know what time and date they're cooking for. We could talk about it after?'

'Okay,' said Leah, 'I'll help you.'

Leah couldn't help but notice that Mo was pleased. It was a subtle shift in his face, like the one she had seen back on their first day when she had given Harold the extra food she had made. There was something about seeing that look of Mo's that made her blush. She stood up quickly from the chair and walked over to the edge of the garden railings. She breathed the hazy summer air and watched as the city prepared for dusk. There was something about the place. It gave her a feeling that just maybe, things were starting to look up.

Chapter 8

~ Reem ~

It had started as one of those ordinary days that your past seems to roll into. A day that began as indistinguishable as the rest. The Tube on that morning ran the same as usual. The bright lights lit up the winding tunnels that were carved underneath the city. Reem arrived at her stop and waited behind the line, watching the train's signal count down the three minutes to its arrival. By the time it was down to one minute, the platform was almost full. As this was her daily commute, she had begun to recognise faces. The same people catching the same train ride every day to get to work on time. The train pulled in and Reem watched the faces of strangers reflected in the glass windows as the carriages slid past. It halted with a screech, pushing a dozen worn commuter bodies into one another. The faint odour of the city, its damp air, smoke and fumes, seemed to taint everyone with the same smell each morning. Reem did her best to avoid being pressed into the others on the carriage, but it was unavoidable. Her five foot and a half inch frame meant she was always under somebody's arm. The train jolted as it pulled off and Reem stood between the two carriage doors so she could look out of the window and down into the tunnel to feel less claustrophobic.

Reem watched through the window as the other passengers shifted between themselves in the carriage opposite, disturbed by someone walking through them. His back was turned to her but she watched him stand close to the back window, about a foot from where she was, but he never once turned around to look. He was watching the other passengers, sidling up close to people in the carriage. There was something about him that intrigued her. His presence felt different to the others she usually saw. He was younger, a slighter build. His clothes weren't the same. They were neither office smart, nor the clinical staple of customer service trades that she was used to wearing. They seemed slightly too small for him, too threadbare for the cold wind outside. His deep auburn hair reached his shoulders and had become wavy, kicking out at the ends despite his obvious efforts to gel it down.

Reem continued to watch him until he disappeared behind a passenger further down the carriage. Just as he slipped from view, he turned to face her. In that brief moment, she saw that his dark brown eyes looked too large in his sunken face. But there was something familiar in them, familiar enough for her to know who he reminded her of. The carriage swayed as it turned and hid him temporarily from Reem's view. She moved her head to try and see from another angle. He reappeared in her view for a couple of seconds. His face disappeared again. But she had seen him long enough for her to realise who he looked like. She stared through the window, trying to get a better view of him. He was almost unrecognisable from the young, carefree boy that would walk to the mosque barefoot and climb the pomegranate tree in their courtyard garden. Suddenly the boy disappeared, swallowed in the suits and bodies, swaying to and fro as the carriage wound its familiar route into the city. The carriage pulled into the next station and

Reem pushed her way off, darted down the platform and jumped onto the adjacent carriage where she had seen the boy. It all happened so quickly that she didn't have time to assess it logically. That from all the searching, she had seen him. Of all the times she had thought she saw him in a crowd, or walking down the street, that each and every time she thought it was Adar, it hadn't been.

People protested as she barged her way through, trying to push her way towards where she had last seen him. Her determination to find out, to see him, to tell him how sorry she was that she had let him down. She had to tell him how she had searched for him since she arrived. People were moaning and muttering under their breath as she pushed through, but she didn't care.

'Adar!' she shouted. A few people turned around and followed her gaze to the boy she was eager to reach. He didn't move.

'Adar, is that you? Adar!'

He turned towards the commotion and looked straight in her eyes. Reem's smile spread across her cheeks. Maybe he didn't recognise her. 'Adar, it's me, Reem.'

The boy looked around, his eyes widened in fear. A brown leather object fell from his hands. A cry of 'thief' echoed around the carriage. The atmosphere was tense. Reem looked around the strangers' faces. None of them made eye contact. They looked down at their feet, moved further down the carriages, scanned through their phones looking for a way to escape. The boy shoved the person next to him and pushed through the crowd. She followed him, passing the brown wallet he had discarded on the floor. Someone picked it up.

'Call the police. He took this,' a passenger in a dark suit said, waving around the wallet in the air. 'He's going to run.'

Some passengers moved further down the carriage away from the scene. Others didn't know what to do and just looked on.

'Someone grab him,' he said, lunging for his collar but missing it as the train braked.

The next station was coming into view. Reem saw him near the doors. She was midway between the carriages. The doors opened and he leapt off onto the platform, falling on his knee as he landed. Reem worked her way down until she was a few metres behind him. He ran in erratic patterns; he knew the station, the exits. He ran into the park. The green landscape stretched in front of her as she watched his figure slowing down, twisting and turning through the trees. The distance between them was increasing. Reem didn't understand why he was running away from her. The disappointment sank through her body and made her legs feel heavy. The pressure in her lungs became painful, her heart quickened. She had forgotten the time; she was far from work, late. Adar had disappeared. The streets resumed their normality. People milled around, fetching breakfast, finishing the last stretch of commute in the mild morning air, cutting though the green opening in the city. The normality of it all made Reem even more devastated. She had never imagined that he would run from her. She remembered his face. His eyes widened in fear. Did he even recognise her?

She rang Mo and spoke uncontrollably, her English becoming mixed with Arabic in her panic.

'I found him but he ran away from me. I think he was stealing from people on the Tube. It was my stupid fault, I shouted his name and now I've lost him again.'

'Woah, slow down, Reem. It's Nidal. Where are you?'

'I don't know. I got off early when the boy did, when Adar did.'

'What can you see?'

'I lost him in St. James' Park, but I haven't been there before, I don't know how to get to work. I don't know if I can even go in now, I –'

'I will get there as soon as I can.'

Reem sat on the bench under the towering trees. The early morning sunlight dappled on the pavement that wound through. A gardener slowly pruned a bush close by, eventually passing her and nodding in acknowledgement. 'Good morning.'

Reem wanted to say it wasn't a good morning. A sharp pain sliced at her heart and filled her with restlessness. Her mind worked furiously to work out how to find him again. Had he been there before? She could do the same commute perhaps and maybe he would be there again. No, he probably wouldn't, she thought to herself as she paced the expanse of soft grass between the trees. Her feet throbbed. She took off her shoes. Her baby wasn't moving inside her. Just as tears began to spill over her cheeks, she saw a figure approaching with a familiar walk. It was Nidal.

He hugged her, albeit a bit awkwardly, but she couldn't withhold the sobs as she leant on his shoulder and she could tell he didn't know what to do.

'Sit down, come on. Sit on this bench.'

Reem followed and wiped her tears away with an old tissue she found crumpled in her pocket, marked with the hotel's name on it.

'I don't wanna upset you, but it wasn't him.'

'It was. He looked different. But it was him.'

'He was nicking someone's wallet. Course he's gonna run.'

'He isn't a thief. He is my brother.'

Nidal kicked at the grass and chewed the side of his lip.

'Now you've calmed down, I'll take you to work. It'll take your mind off it.'

Reem didn't have any more energy to protest and she knew she needed the money, now more than ever. It wasn't like she had a clean record since starting. She never seemed to get anything right. As Nidal walked next to her, her mind flashed a series of images into her head. In the images, the boy shifted into the different faces she had met in her life. Faces of those she had known back home, new faces that passed through the hotel where she worked. She tried to cling onto the moment where he had turned to face her, when his eyes met hers. She had seen something in them in that second, a feeling of familiarity, like he had known her. But he looked different, like he wasn't her baby brother anymore. Surely that was because he was older and was turning into a young man. But soon the face she saw became a blur in the crowd, until she was certain she wouldn't recognise him even if he was stood right in front of her.

'Did you hear me?'

'Sorry Nidal, no.'

'We can chat about it another time. You don't seem ready.'

Reem knew her voice was void of any emotion, but she felt as she had after he had first gone missing, like she had been planted in another realm where her feet barely touched the floor. It was only temporary, she had thought.

Like the insomnia, the partial amnesia. She used to know the earth was temporary. Back when her days were spent gazing at the open sky, peering through it for cracks to show a hint of what lay above; the promised paradise that had guided her and kept her focused. She used to be soothed by it. But in a city where she spent so much time underground, where she worked cleaning the dirt and secrets off the sheets, in a city where the buildings towered in the sky, she had all but forgotten.

She reached the station and wandered down the steps, leaving Nidal behind. If she had turned around, she would have seen him pacing back and forth, following her footsteps then retracing them outside on the street, watching her walking away and then deciding to let her go, his figure shrunken against a sullen sky. If she had known then how it would be, how due to Nidal the truth would come, how through him the world would learn her secret, she might have given him more of her time. If she'd have known the price that truth would come at, she might have warned him not to get close to her. But of course, no one was to know. Not even him.

chapter 9

~ Leah ~

Leah started to settle into her routine. She also spent time reviewing the local schools and now wasn't so opposed to the idea of Elijah attending. Elijah seemed better; he was finding his way and becoming his own person outside of the organised schedules he had flitted between before. Brianna told her which school she had attended, and Leah was impressed at how she had thrived. It gave her confidence that Elijah could too. Her mum had said they would pay for Elijah's school but since she hadn't been forthcoming about handing over the cheques, Leah wasn't sure what conditions she would attach to it. Jane was also visiting regularly and since it was the topic she always asked about, Leah decided to register him.

The apartment, now it was decluttered and kept clean, was spacious enough for the two of them. The living area was a decent size and the bedrooms looked so much better with a fresh coat of paint. Elijah displayed his treasures on his new bedroom shelf and she enjoyed creating a sanctuary in her room. She piled up her new collection of books next to the bed. They opened up new ideas they could share together; beekeeping, gardening on a budget, creating an Asian garden in the UK. The world had grown bigger; it had stretched and allowed them to enjoy it in ways they hadn't before. She had so much more to learn, so much more she could teach Elijah. His natural curiosity about anything and everything, and his free time to explore meant he was beginning to thrive. It made him more independent and he was happier. Leah decided that she was going to spend the next few weeks just enjoying their time together – something she had not done for a long time.

Elijah woke up each morning eager to see how his planted date seeds were growing and he kept some pots spare for when he had the pomegranate seeds. They watered and fed the plants and Leah loved being out in the summer air, with the city view below her as Elijah created his own space in previously unused parts of the courtyard. It was like their own patch of goodness amongst the concrete.

Mo went to visit Laila after Reem tipped her off about the pomegranate seeds. She poured them into four paper cups and Mo delivered them to Elijah. None of them had any idea how they would work, but Elijah tested them by planting pots in different areas of the garden using different types of compost and Leah found a page in her book about making mini greenhouses to emulate the heat, but with the scorching summer heatwave, they all agreed they probably didn't need one. It was winter that would be difficult, but with it being a long way off, they hadn't given it any further thought. The winter gloom was as distant as the universe that was surrounding them.

Emily's beekeeper came to visit the eighth floor garden. He gave it a quick assessment and asked to see the roof as hives tended to be better suited to the roof of buildings so as not to disturb the residents. They explained the elevator wasn't currently working so he gave up on that idea, and gave them a proposal for a hive in the far right corner of the garden. That was going to be the dedicated area. To make sure that it was suitable, they would need to plant more flowers and install a screen to protect the hive and the residents. Leah and Mo agreed, and within the following days, it was set up on the roof. There was a lot of interest around the hive. A few new members joined the gardening club and most of the current members brought extra wild flowers, along with a few experimental ones to see if they would eventually be able to taste the difference in the honey. The flowers blossomed and the bees stayed in the hive.

There were a couple of protective suits so that they could harvest the honey and Elijah really wanted to get close to have a look. Leah kept thinking of anaphylactic shock and how the bees surrounded him in her night-mares, but with the specialist suit and Mo's supervision, she let him get close. She felt sick just watching them, es-pecially as the bees became disturbed and began to rise up from the hive to see what was going on. It took everything she had to remain calm. When Mo and Elijah emerged, he was as excited as the bees. Leah saw under his arm, where he was scratching. He had been stung.

'Stick out your tongue.'

'What?'

'Open your mouth and stick out your tongue. I need to see if there's any swelling.'

'Mum, please, I'm fine. It's just a bit itchy.'

Leah had the EpiPen on standby, clenched in her fist.

'Does he have an allergy?' said Mo, pointing to the EpiPen.

'No, not that I know of.'

'So you keep that just in case?'

'You can never be too careful when it comes to kids.'

Mo laughed, although he suppressed it so quickly that Leah was sure it was just a jerk reaction.

'He's a little man, Leah. You have to let go of the reins a bit sometimes.'

She knew Mo was right, but it was so difficult for her. Exhausting, even. She put the EpiPen away, realising she could probably leave it at home now.

Elijah's summer holidays were in full swing. They learnt the art of beekeeping together and began to enjoy their time out on the garden, spending time there in the evenings. Even Leah began to relax. The vivid dreams of Matthew had calmed down and the nightmares about the bees had stopped. She concentrated on the days of summer they had together. Leah saw how separate she had been from him and had begun to appreciate him in ways that she couldn't before. She noticed he had become taller and his face was losing the look he had as a child. She increasingly saw Matthew in him. She saw it in his cheekbones that appeared once the baby fat had gone, in the way he ruffled his hair with his fingers, and the way his tongue touched his upper lip when he was concentrating.

She appreciated how he was so passionate about his little world. He took her to see all the discoveries he had made and even gave her his pyrite, his most prized piece of golden treasure. In return, Leah found him more crystals. She knew that scientifically speaking they were just rock formations that had formed over thousands of years, but to Elijah they were magical pieces of the earth. Everything that hid under its surface was proof that it held secrets to discover. He found treasure everywhere. He would stand on rubbish heaps and the mound beneath him would morph into the body of a sunken pirate ship or an ancient palace buried beneath its surface. All Leah could see was broken glass, stones and rubbish.

In a strange way, the change of scenery and the new community helped her to feel as though life was beginning for them both. She saw he was happier here with Reem and Mo. He hadn't had any episodes since they had moved, maybe because he now shared his life with others. Others who, until now, appreciated what Leah couldn't.

Leah was also able to take him around London to visit his favourite places; all the places they wouldn't have time to go to when school restarted in a few weeks. She had been so busy before with her medical training that Matthew had done most things with Elijah. She had missed out on it, and then when he died, grief took over. Reem mentioned that she had stumbled upon the Natural History Museum and Leah remembered that Elijah hadn't been since he was young, so they visited there and spent ages looking at the dinosaur bones whilst Elijah jotted down notes about the different eras of the dinosaurs. He took along the pieces he had found over the last few months and tried to see if he could see any matches with those that were on display. He even managed to find a particularly friendly member of staff who had a keen look at them and delighted in telling him that, although he couldn't be sure, he thought they did look like the bones of a raptor.

Her cleaning shifts were more regular than she expected, so sometimes she would drop Elijah off to his grandparents' house and other times, Mo or Reem would look after him. Emily changed Leah's schedule by leaving a note with her payment. She had thought it was slightly odd that she hadn't seen Emily again since she walked in on her by mistake. They had regular parties but Leah never received any invites. She had stopped caring. It wasn't the fact that she wasn't invited that hurt, but how people scattered the moment things fell apart.

Leah was almost finished on this particular occasion when she swung open a bedroom door, expecting to find an empty hospital bed. She let out a squeal, dropping the polish in her hands.

'Blimey, are you trying to give me a heart attack?' an old man said, laying his head back down on the pillow.

'I'm so sorry! I will leave you to it,' Leah said, remembering how Emily had told her about Ray's dad, Arnold. It must have been him.

'You may as well come in now. I've been listening to your singing all afternoon,' he said dryly.

Leah rubbed so hard she could have polished a hole through the dresser, trying to avoid eye contact.

'I didn't think you were here. I thought you were at the Mews?'

'Yes, charming isn't it, that they brought me home to die in my old house.'

'Oh, I thought it was...' Leah stopped, realising how intrusive it sounded.

'No, you can say it. They've been partying ever since they took it from beneath my feet. You know how much of my career I spent building for a home like this, only to have it snatched away whilst I'm still alive? And ungratefully at that, too.'

Leah carried on dusting, trying to avoid any more conversation.

'And that, out the window.'

Leah followed his finger, pointing towards the building she lived in.

'A constant reminder.'

Leah didn't want to ask what he meant. She thought she already knew. She had already heard before how the building was an eyesore that dragged down house prices and how it should be demolished and rebuilt on the outskirts of the capital.

'Here, let me show you something.'

He struggled to sit up, so Leah instinctively went over to help.

'Pass me those under the bed,' Arnold said, leaning off and jabbing his finger to point towards a roll of papers that were pushed underneath. Leah pulled them up.

'Open them for me.'

Leah spread them out on the bed. They were architect's drawings of a building.

'You see, my whole life was spent working on building something, a paradise for people to live in. It was going to be revolutionary.'

'Sounds impressive.'

'That's what I thought. I dedicated all my time to it. I worked day and night as though it was my very own baby, from conception. I thought it would be the making of me.'

He lay back down. The exuberance in his eyes faded.

'What is it?'

'Back when this place wasn't as rich as it is now, well, slowly the money filtered in and pushed up the house prices. They saw a use for these high-rise buildings, you see. It freed up the houses for the ones who could afford it, but they needed somewhere cheaper for the rest.'

'People need places to live in. Have you ever been inside?'

'Once, years ago. And now I can't see what it has become. I can barely get out of this bed. All I see is the windows. Dark windows and nothing behind them.'

Leah remembered what Emily had said about the onset of his dementia.

'Now look at me. I don't even own the house I'm dying in. Even the bed I'm lying on doesn't belong to me.'

'Here, let me get you comfortable.'

'That was my problem. I was too comfortable. And now no one thinks I'm making any sense when everything is perfectly clear. My whole life has passed, eighty-eight long years, yet it feels as though they have been spent in a morning, or an afternoon. And what have they amounted to?'

Leah looked back at the drawings. 'This would have been a wonderful place to live. I can see it.'

He pointed out of the window.

'What is it?'

'That's it.'

'What?'

'That is the building. That was supposed to be my dream but all it does is haunt me. Concession after concession it changed, until it grew into something I had no control over.'

'I think it's a great building.' Leah paused. 'I'm very happy there. Me and my son.'

'You mean to say you live there?'

Lead nodded, smiling.

'Tell me all about it. Make me see inside.'

Leah proceeded to tell him about how her home there had been a healer for her and her son. How the garden space was growing beautifully and how they now had bees making honey.

His eyes were closing. 'Yes, I've seen the bees. Sometimes I think I can hear them.'

She told him that the windows gave one of the best views over the city she had ever seen, how the floor space was larger than most new builds, and now that it was getting a facelift, would transform the cityscape.

'Maybe I could move there. Be rid of this place.'

Leah didn't respond. She let him whisper words in his delirium as he dropped in and out of sleep until he finally stopped.

Relieved, she rolled up the plans and placed them back under the bed. She left quietly, leaving the door slightly ajar. She ran downstairs and out into the fresh air. Free.

***

The day of their community *iftar* was approaching. Elijah and Leah went to the local library and printed out posters and invitations templates from the Big Iftar website that Elijah had found online. The library stalls were quiet, and whilst they were waiting for the posters to be printed, Elijah and Leah scanned the books, looking for some to take home with them. Leah found a new recipe book for Turkish food which reminded her that Mo said he might not be able to afford to go to the Turkish restaurant this Ramadan. As she flicked through the pages she thought the recipes looked delicious and not too hard, which was important as she was nervous about her cooking. Mary, her mum's house helper and her old nanny, had always made the dinners at home and never allowed Leah to help in the kitchen. Then when she got married, Matthew took over. Although she had learnt a few recipes from him, she had never really learned to cook herself or really knew what she liked. Now she had the time and an occasion, she had the book stamped and began to plan her meal. She knew Mo said she didn't have to cook, but she wanted to.

They left the library after the librarian agreed they could pin up one of their posters there. She and Elijah went around the local community advertising the event, knocking on people's doors and inviting their neighbours. For those that didn't answer, she slipped a leaflet under the door. The neighbours who were involved could bring dishes down on the date they had set, and those who didn't want to cook were invited anyway.

Finishing up, they arrived home and Leah opened the door to their apartment. The sun streamed through the glass windows and warmed the place up. She curled up on the sofa with Elijah and he read his book whilst she read hers. There were so many things she would have liked to try.

She saved the pages of the lamb, cauliflower and chickpea stew, the minced koftas in pitta bread and stuffed aubergine with feta.

'Elijah, what do you think about these?' she said, turning the pages and showing him the pictures.

'Ooh they look delicious, mummy. Are they for us?'

'Well, you can eat them too, but I'm thinking for the Big *Iftar*.'

Elijah took the book and reread the pages. 'Lamb though, mummy. It has to be *halal*.'

'Oh,' Leah said, 'where do I get halal meat from? Does it taste different?'

'No, mum, it doesn't. Mo took me last week. The meat tastes the same. It's just how they kill the animal that's different. The butcher on the corner does *halal*. I can show you if you want?'

'That would be lovely, darling, thank you.' Leah beamed and stroked his hair as he skipped straight to the dessert page.

'Wow, look at these,' he said, pointing to the Turkish delight recipe. 'Have I ever had Turkish delight before?'

'No, I don't think you have,' Leah said, looking at the ingredient list: sugar, cornflour, rose essence and a pinch of cream of tartar. 'I think we could make this together if you like?'

'Yeah, let's do it. Finish off our Turkish themed dinner.'

'Great!'

'Why did you choose Turkish, mummy?'

'Oh, I just fancied it. It looks yummy doesn't it?'

Elijah nodded and flicked through the recipe book so quickly Leah knew he wasn't reading it. Leah wondered if he had seen straight through to her secret.

***

On the day of the *iftar*, they decided to make lamb koftas and a cauliflower and chickpea stew, followed by Elijah's choice of Turkish delight. They headed to the kitchen at the community centre where the regular women who worked there had been busy preparing the food since the morning. Ayesha had been making food for refugees for the past few years in the kitchens there. She was older than Leah, in her late thirties, and always wore a signature green headscarf of varying shades. She welcomed them into the kitchen, rolling up the sleeves on her top, and carried half the shopping from Leah's hands. Leah placed all her ingredients on the side and they began making the koftas. Leah leaned the recipe book against the tea and sugar pots, hoping it wouldn't get splashed with food as they cooked.

Elijah stirred the bowl of minced meat and added the spices one by one using a teaspoon. 'Are you sure six teaspoons of garam masala, Myriam, it seems a lot.'

'We're feeding a lot!' said Myriam, tying her headscarf around the back of her neck so it stayed out of the way of the spices.

'What's that picture on your apron?' Elijah said.

'That's where I am from, Jerusalem. It's the Dome of the Rock. It's famous.'

'That looks cool, is that real gold?'

'Gold plated I think,' said Myriam.

'Bring me some back when you next visit!' Elijah said, excitedly.

'I can't go back.'

'How come?'

'It's a long story and for now we have an *iftar* to cook. Do you think you can add these onions?'

Elijah added the onions Leah had been crying over as she chopped them. Under Myriam's experienced eye, he then added the crushed garlic and coriander. 'Smell this, mummy, it smells delicious,' Elijah said, leaning over the large bowl.

Leah came over and inhaled deeply over the pan. 'Mmm, it does. You're doing a great job. Think I'll leave you to it whilst I get started on the Turkish delight. There aren't lots of ingredients but I'm pretty sure boiling sugar to that consistency will take a while and we can't be late!'

Leah went over to the stove and boiled the sugar, stirring it until it was thick enough to form balls when dropped into water. She then mixed the cornflour and cream of tartar in another saucepan and heated it, stirring continuously whilst it thickened into a gloop.

Meanwhile, Elijah began to roll out the kebab patties and was lining them up on a baking tray to put them in the oven. As the oven was small, they would need to do at least four batches to get them all cooked. Leah alternated between stirring the cornflour mixture and sliding the koftas into the oven. The building was hot and smelt like a Turkish kitchen. Elijah was busy humming away to himself as he used a butter knife to open up the pittas and slid in one piece of washed lettuce, a ring of onion and a slice of tomato.

Eventually the cornflour mixture and the sugar were mixed together and Leah added pink food colouring and rose essence. She then greased a square dish and lined it with parchment paper before pouring the mixture in. When it had solidified, she turned it out into a blend of icing sugar and cornflour and cut it up into cubes.

'Wow, it looks like the real thing! Can I try it?'

'Yes, sure,' Leah said, waiting eagerly for the response, hoping after all this time it at least tasted edible. 'Here, let me have some,' she said, unable to resist taking a cube of her hard work and letting it melt on her tongue.

'It's good, I knew it would be. Good job, mum.'

'And look at these that you made!' Leah said, looking at the trays lined up with koftas stuffed inside a pitta, complete with salad and a dollop of mint yoghurt.

'I think we have just found a new dinner for us!'

'Oh no,' said Leah, looking at the time, 'I forgot the veggie option, the chickpea and cauliflower stew!'

'How long does it take to make it?' Elijah said, turning the recipe book pages until he found it. 'It says half an hour to cook so we have plenty of time. I'll help.'

'We can help too,' two of the women said, looking over the ingredients.

Myriam chopped up the cauliflower and Leah was thankful someone else had brought re-soaked chickpeas as the dried ones she had bought needed to be soaked for twenty-four hours in advance. Ayesha chopped the onion, garlic, crushed tomatoes and a similar spice mix that they used for the koftas, before adding it to the pan with some vegetable stock and leaving it to simmer.

'It says you should roast the cauliflower but I'm sure it will be just as nice if we fry it off and let it cook in the stew for half an hour,' Myriam said.

'Yeah, I don't like my veg too soggy,' Elijah said.

'Since when do you like veg anyway?' Leah laughed.

'This I will definitely eat, it smells yummy.'

'Come on then, you need to get changed.' Leah looked up and down at Elijah and herself. 'We're covered in food and spices!'

'Like proper chefs,' Ayesha said.

She moved half of the food onto the table and the Turkish delight was cut up on a large chopping board and placed into smaller pots. Myriam served the stew in the big saucepan she had washed already.

'Yes, we look and smell like we work in the best Turkish restaurant!' Leah laughed.

'Maybe I will be a chef when I grow up. It's fun.'

'Why not, baby? You can do whatever you want.'

And this time, as Leah tidied up and washed the pots with Myriam and Ayesha, she thought to herself that she actually meant it. She didn't feel any pressure that he had to be a certain way. He didn't need a specialist school background or a lucrative career. He was perfect, just the way he was.

Chapter 10

~ *Reem* ~

Reem's days at work helped the time to pass a lot easier than when she was at home. As Reem was working and seeing the midwife regularly, Jane wasn't too concerned about her more infrequent visits and Reem felt better not having her visit her at the apartment. She had gradually brought her collection out of the kitchen cupboard and began to place them around the room again, as some people would have done with photos. For Reem, they were the snapshots of her history.

The hotel work in the back area was more suited to her and became somewhat of a blessing because she had found a practically unused store room filled with soaps, shampoos and other toiletries, and she managed to make her prayers there. She would go on her break and sometimes, when Kesandu was there, she would keep watch at the door. It was in those quiet moments when Reem was praying, her forehead touching the floor, that she would feel the most secure. It gave her a sense of calm amidst the madness. The pace slowed down and she reconnected with Allah, and with the roots she left behind. When she was kneeling on her prayer mat with her forehead pressed to the floor, she could have been anywhere in the world and it no longer mattered where that was. She sometimes thought she smelt the aroma of musk seeping up from the clean sheet she lay on the floor to pray on. She imagined she was praying on the indigo-coloured carpet that quilted the mosque floor back home.

There were many differences between this Ramadan and the Ramadans back home. Here she felt the absence of it through the everyday routines, through the people she met; it was strange to her that the days felt normal, not special in the way they did when shared with her family and neighbours. The fasts were easy since she scarcely thought of food anymore. Although it wasn't incumbent on her to fast since she was pregnant, she felt it was necessary in the absence of Adar. She couldn't enjoy the comfort of food and water; an expiation for her sins.

It was the sumptuous breaking of the fast that she struggled with. She had avoided it as most evenings she was by herself at home. The streets didn't change, no one knocked on her door with food. When dusk came and she was still on her shift, she would pull out the couple of dates she had brought to work and drink water, breaking her fast alone. It was nothing like she was used to, but she had control over what she did and it made her feel like the days were not wasted as she tried to rack up goodness in her life. The focus of Ramadan made her want to do more. The thirty days of the month had helped her to reconnect with her faith. This year, she could use it to try to make up for her lost time and she saw it as an opportunity to try and turn her life around. She didn't worry so much as her mind was preoccupied with her body's basic needs. She spent the evenings eating food that nourished her body and her baby. She barely slept, waking up half an hour before dawn to eat breakfast before the sun rose. A breakfast that had to sustain her until the long day ended. She didn't always make it to dusk, but it was enough to make her feel that she was trying, that her life was moving forward.

The Tube journey had ended and the streets seemed quiet. She walked the short distance to the squares surrounded by the tower block. She barely recognised it. The usually empty patch of grass in front of the building had been transformed. Around the edges of the grass, poles with bunting and fairy lights were strung all around the grass. Running down the centre were long strips of carpets, blankets and rugs and placed on top of them were multiple dishes of food. The aroma of steaming rice, meat and various curries danced in the air.

Reem could barely count all the people that were there. She noticed Mo, Nidal, Brianna, Chantelle and Bill; Leah and Elijah were there with them too. Either side of them people sat and ate, creating two long lines opposite each other, sharing the food in the centre. She couldn't help comparing it to the *iftars* she had at home, where family, friends and neighbours would gather outside to eat together as dusk fell. Young and old, poor and rich. Everyone held open invites at their homes, their courtyard gates flung open, their patios lit up in the dark, inviting people in from the streets to share their meals in celebration of breaking the fast. As a child, she would stay up late, and she and Mahmoud would sneak off and roam the old city that became theirs under the moonlight.

'Reem, come look what I made!' Elijah shouted from the crowd.

Reem went and sat by Elijah and Leah. 'Delicious, my favourite now. You can come and cook for me in the week,' Reem said, licking yoghurt from her fingers. 'Who organised this?'

'We all did,' said Mo.

'Mostly Mo and Leah,' said Nidal, nudging him with his elbow.

'It takes everyone to get involved to pull it off,' Mo said, gesturing to the food and dishes that the neighbours had brought and were now sharing.

'Ayesha and Myriam too. I couldn't have done it without them,' Leah said, gesturing to them down the middle of the runner.

Mo stood up. 'We should pray *magrib*.'

'Prayer time for anyone who wants to join us!' Nidal shouted down the dinner line as Mo began the call to prayer in Arabic.

Reem listened to the soft dulcet tones of his Arabic in an accent she hadn't heard. It was melodious and filled the sky with the old sounds of her home. She closed her eyes and imagined the mosques' minarets towering above them, between the tower blocks and breaking up the monotonous expanse of grey.

People left the banquet and climbed over dishes, rinsed their mouths and hands, some of the women tied their hair back into scarves and they gathered together to join Mo at the front as Reem watched him lead them in prayers. The men and women bowing in unison and the recitation of the Qur'an made her fall in love again with its reminders, its simplicity. It rooted her to what she believed in, where she came from, and where she was headed.

'Why do they all face that direction?' Leah asked.

'Muslims pray towards Mecca in Saudi Arabia.'

'Oh, I thought it was Jerusalem.'

'Actually, it used to be. But it changed after Prophet Muhammad came.'

'Mo seems to be very keen on organising things around here, I've noticed,' Leah said.

'Yes, I guess so,' said Reem, 'but you seem to be very involved in the community yourself. And you made Turkish Delight, hey? We know someone said they liked Turkish food...'

'What's that supposed to mean?'

'I wonder if there's another reason you chose this,' said Reem, nudging her arm.

'I don't like him like that, if that's what you are getting at.' Leah turned her face away and started shuffling plates around and throwing empty ones into a bin liner round the edge of the table, before giving up and sitting back down. 'It doesn't matter anyway. He practically runs away from me every time I go near him.'

Reem laughed. 'I wouldn't take it personally.'

'What do you mean?' Leah said, sitting down next to her.

'Well, because of his religion, he can't be alone with you or touch you in any way. You aren't married to him and you certainly aren't his sister.'

'So that's why he backs off, in case I go to kiss or hug him?'

Reem laughed. 'You and your air kissing everyone you meet.'

'Hey!' said Leah, throwing her napkin at her. 'I was just being friendly. What about a handshake?'

'Nope.'

'Anything?'

'No, not unless you're his wife. Then you can do whatever you want.' Reem couldn't help but giggle again and it made Leah smile.

'Oh yes, I just remembered my mum has invited you over for dinner. As a way of apologising for when you met back at the hotel.'

Reem had to think for a second. 'Really?'

Leah nodded. 'Wait a minute, someone's missing.'

'Who?'

'Just hold on.'

Reem watched Leah go inside. A few minutes later, she was practically dragging Harold outside to come and join them. He sat down and after Leah had given him a plate, he scooped up a bit of everything and began to eat.

Reem glanced around and felt happiness surge through her bones for the first time in a long time. She couldn't believe how many people had come to celebrate. She saw all the people who lived their lives behind closed doors, who were now out in the open in the fresh air, sharing the same sky. For that brief moment, they were one.

***

Reem was still brimming with the feeling that just maybe her life was about to turn a corner. If she hadn't been preoccupied, she might have noticed the wood splintered around the door frame. She might have noticed that she hadn't left the lights on inside. As the door creaked open, she saw a figure standing there by the window. For a moment, Reem thought she had walked into the wrong flat.

He was standing there with his back to her, with her stolen artefact in his fingers. When he turned around she saw it was a face she recognised, one she thought she had left firmly in the past, between a distance of oceans that she hoped he would never cross. But suddenly, the earth felt smaller. A slice of what she had tried to hide from her old life had walked straight into her new one.

She could tell by his face that Nazim was revelling in his unexpected visit, in the fear that it brought to her body. She hated that she couldn't hide it from him. He didn't break the silence. He wouldn't, she thought. He would let this last as long as he could. He was like that. She had seen it before when she was back home and it was all falling apart and they came to him, desperate. That was when serenity replaced his malice – for a brief second when he knew that he could have whatever he wanted. That was how he had amassed his fortune.

'What are you doing here?'

'That is the greeting a husband reunited with his wife gets, after all this time? I thought you would be pleased that I too, escaped.'

Reem didn't have any concerns about him dying. The war profited him so much that she wasn't surprised that he thrived whilst the rest of the country crumbled.

'I am pleased. I'm just shocked because I didn't expect to see you.'

'So I need an invitation now, do I?'

'No, I didn't mean that –'

Reem stared at his frame as he hunched over the artefact, gripping it in his hand, raising it slightly to the light. His old, crooked frame looked fatter. The meat around his bones had padded him out, making him look more youthful than his fifty odd years. She had never asked how old he was. She understood her parents' deal, and his age wasn't relevant. He ran his tanned hand, paler than it had been before, through his slightly greasy black hair that clung with all its might to the sides of his head.

Reem took a few steps backwards out the door. Adrenaline had been pumping around her veins and it had reached its peak. She could outrun him. He wouldn't be able to catch her. London was different. There were places she could go. She had seen leaflets back at the Town Hall about it. She could get help. Leah had told her that her life could be different.

'I wouldn't plan on running, Reem. After all, where would you go? Who would want a used up thief like you?'

'I wasn't –'

She felt a fool for ever thinking she could escape from him. He turned around, his smile spreading across his face like a disease. She noticed he limped slightly in his left leg as he came towards her. He couldn't move it properly. She stared at it, unable to tear her eyes away from the weakness she had never seen in him before.

'Did you hear me, you thief? After everything I have done for you, you steal from me?'

He brought his hand down and sharply struck her across the cheek.

'If it wasn't for you carrying my child, I would have no further use for you.'

Reem stood with her face stinging. His presence took up all the space in the apartment. 'Now go and find me something to eat.'

'It's late, I am not sure anywhere –'

'Do what I tell you and don't answer me back.'

Reem turned around, relieved to get out into the hallway. As she turned she saw him standing at her door. 'And don't think about going anywhere. I can find you here. I will find you again and next time, I won't be so generous.'

Reem's heart beat so loudly she could hear it coming out of her chest. She hurried down the staircase and out into the night. The night was still. There weren't many people around. It wasn't like Ramadan back home where during the nights, the streets and the markets would come alive. Whole families would be out enjoying the cooler weather, breaking their fasts at buffet restaurants, visiting neighbours with trays of sweets, trying out delicacies made especially for Ramadan in the sweet shops and finishing their evenings by shopping for Eid gifts. Here, she couldn't see another person outside. Lights glowed from inside the windows, and she wondered if behind the curtains other families were celebrating. She glanced up at the moon, kneeling down on the damp grass. Please find me a way out of this, she pleaded with her hands cupped to the sky. If there was any time her prayers would be answered, Ramadan was that time. She picked herself up and dusted the grass off her clothes. The fresh spring smell of cut grass transported her back home, reminding her of when she was a young girl. She had been scared to leave that evening when her father had asked her to take Adar to the grocery store. He knelt next to her and said, 'You can't live your life in fear, Reem.' She couldn't remember what else he had said, but that was how she had always felt; like deep down something was lurking behind everything she loved, waiting to snatch it away.

Reem shopped at the tiny convenience store around the corner. It was the only shop open at this time and as her eyes scanned the produce, mostly tins and cans and some dried goods, her heart dropped. She couldn't make anything that he would accept out of what was there.

She rushed home to prepare rice and lentils and served it with green beans and the okra she had left in the fridge. Nazim ate furiously as though he hadn't eaten in weeks. Once he had finished, his attention turned back to Reem. He pressed his hand on her stomach.

'You are lucky this baby is here. If it wasn't for you carrying my baby, you wouldn't have been worth the price.'

He fell asleep on the sofa, his head titled back, his mouth wide open. Reem looked at him sprawled out, invading her home. He had brought with him an old suitcase, half open and stuffed with clothes, as though he had left in a hurry.

Reem had barely slept when Nazim woke up, demanding breakfast.

'I'm sorry, I forgot to wake you for *suhour*. I didn't wake up myself. I –'

'What are you talking about?' Nazim said, his face creased into a frown,

'*Suhour*, the food before dawn so we can fast for the day.'

'Don't talk to me like I'm an idiot. I know what *suhour* is. Make me some food.'

Reem didn't ask anything else. She didn't want to assume that he had forgotten it was Ramadan. Maybe he didn't have to fast because he was on medication or was suffering from ill health. Either way, she wasn't going to press him any further.

She went to the fridge and pulled out a pack of eggs. Nazim came behind her and breathed over her as she peered in the fridge trying to think of what to make him, whilst her heart raced. His breath made her feel nauseous.

'You made me eggs on our wedding morning.'

Reem forced her mouth into a smile, but it became more of a grimace.

'You remember?' Nazim said, his hands wrapping around her waist like a serpent tightening its grip.

'You must be hungry. Let me make you some food,' Reem said, sliding past and knocking the saucepans around in the high cupboard, forcing Nazim to move away from the falling pans. 'Sorry, it's a small kitchen.'

Nazim skulked off and sat at the small table. Reem could feel his eyes burrowing into the back of her as she cooked. She felt sick to the stomach.

'You looked so much younger on our wedding day. I thought I had married a twenty-year-old?'

'I was twenty then.'

'And yet it was only a year ago. How time flies by. To imagine, I've known you since you were young.'

Reem nodded, unable to speak. She did remember. She remembered how girls weren't allowed to go into his shop by themselves. His own nieces weren't allowed to visit his house without their father. Suspicions hung over him as readily as his eyes peered from his shop windows at the girls walking by. The bell on the door rang out into the street as he tried to call them in to see the latest jewellery he had acquired. Dowry, he called it. He had done it to Reem once when she was at college. She was barely sixteen. She felt guilty ignoring him when he called her name out.

'Come here, Reem. I have something for you.'

She turned to look around her on the empty street and saw no one. Her brain didn't work fast enough to give her a reason.

'My father's expecting me, Nazim. I have to go.'

'Come, just for a minute.' He was closer, his hands reaching out for her arm.

She yanked it free and kicked his ankle, feeling empowered, free from his grip. She knew he hadn't forgotten. Every time she saw him afterwards she saw his injured pride, barely concealed in the shortness of his breath, the way he watched her like a hyena waiting to snatch prey.

'I remember the nights before you left. Do you remember them, Reem?' Nazim said, sighing deeply as he rested in the chair. 'I waited a long time for you. You looked so modest on our wedding day. Do you remember what a good day that was? How many people came?'

She remembered how her old friends had sullen faces and only minutes before she appeared at the wedding party, had urged her to run away. She remembered how she felt. How everyone must have known that she didn't want to marry him, but when there is war, there is no choice. In wars, people don't marry for love. People marry for survival. She remembered walking down towards him. Her body shaking with a sickness that had gripped her since she had agreed to it. Every muscle in her body was fighting against walking towards him. But then amidst the music and the perfumed smell of flowers and the overpowering *oud* that hung in the air, she turned and saw Adar's face in the crowd. He smiled at her, beaming. She could do this, she thought, and committed to Nazim in spite of it all.

'This country has aged you.'

'Maybe it was the journey.'

Nazim's tone switched. 'No, I think it's your attitude. You have been left to your own devices with no one to keep you in check and now you look haggard.'

She had forgotten he didn't like to be disagreed with. She swallowed hard, and realised her hand was shaking as she served up his eggs, accompanied with creamy yoghurt and a small plate of withered looking olives. She hoped it would be good enough. He held her hand.

'Steady now,' he said, his smirk creeping up through the stubble on his cheeks. 'Aren't you going to join me?'

'I'm going to try and fast today.'

'Sit. You don't have to fast. You need to eat and feed my child.'

'I've been okay. I eat well all through the night and usually at *suhour* too. The doctor said it's okay as long as I do that. If I don't feel well, I just break my fast early.'

'It wasn't a question. Eat.' Nazim shoved a plate in front of her nose and then slammed it onto the table, making her jump.

Reem sat down and scooped up some egg with her bread. Her mouth was dry and she was almost unable to swallow it. The baby kicked hard in her stomach. Her stomach tightened.

'There, that's better. My son needs his strength.'

'Your son?'

'I always knew I'd have a son first.'

She was at least relieved when Nazim went out on what he called "business errands". Reem paced around the house, cleaning up the pots from breakfast and the ones she had left last night. Too exhausted, too off balance to consider doing anything, she had just climbed into bed and hoped he would go away. She tidied the apartment and made Nazim some dinner for when he returned. It was the night Leah had invited her for the dinner party. She knew Nazim would be angry if she wasn't there when she returned but she didn't know what would happen if she stayed and she didn't want to find out. She left the cooked dinner in a pot with a handwritten note saying she was at work. She headed for the Tube station and glanced back at the tower, praying that when she returned, that by some miracle, he would be gone.

Chapter 11

~ Leah ~

Leah arrived reluctantly but at least Reem was there to keep her company. She couldn't understand why Reem was so thankful to be there since she herself had tried to avoid the ghastly dinner parties since she left. At least Elijah seemed happy to go.

'Are you sure you want to go? You really don't have to,' Leah asked as they stood at the door.

Reem seemed distracted. 'I want to. It reminds me of when I was young. We would host these parties and I loved them.'

Leah forced a smile. She loved Reem's innocence most of the time but sometimes it worried her that she could be so detached. It was a symptom Leah had seen before.

Mary opened the door and her mum stood there, dressed in swathes of sick-coloured peach.

'Ophelia, Elijah, my darling. So wonderful to see you.'

'Hi mum, this is Reem. You met at the hotel the other day.'

Leah's mother stopped and looked her up and down, revealing a smile that she saved for her best staff.

'Of course. Why, what a beautiful dress. It almost looks like you made it yourself.'

'I did,' said Reem.

'How delightful.'

Leah followed her mum inside, hoping Reem didn't feel out of place. The dining room was set for dinner and the garden doors were open at the back allowing it to feel less claustrophobic than it usually did, owing to it being packed full of furniture and ornate crystalware and china. Everything her mum had bought was on display. The people standing on the patio outside the doors turned around. She noticed Charles straight away. He was a burly figure, hard to miss. He kept his meek, brown hair cut sharply around his ears, giving him the look of a retired military officer. He spoke first.

'Ophelia, how long has it been since we saw you around this neighbourhood?'

Great, thought Leah, straight to the point. She didn't have the right postcode and the comment had to come from Charles. She hadn't liked him since she first met him.

'Don't listen to him, Ophelia. We are just pleased to see you both and erm...' His wife, Stella, had a way of softening his comments, or they would never have been invited back to most of the places they went. Stella stroked her sleek bob of ginger hair and looked more relaxed in her rose print blouse and navy trousers, pressed with a crease running exactly down the centre of them.

'Sorry, this is Reem. She's my friend.'

'Reem... hey, that's an Arabic name, I believe. Where are you from?' Reem went to speak but Charles interrupted again. 'Let me guess,' he said, his eyes creeping over her. 'Syria. Yes, I am sure of it. Spent some time there myself.'

'What did you do there?' Reem asked, wondering if he had something to do with the army.

'Just a bit of consulting business.'

'But you're a surgeon, Charles?' Leah asked inquisitively.

'Leave the poor girls alone, Charles. Honestly! Come on, let's get you outside for some fresh air.'

When Charles and his wife went outside, Leah faced her mum and said, 'So I see Charles is sozzled before we've even had dinner – once again.'

'Oh don't be so judgmental, Ophelia. He's going through hard times.'

Leah rolled her eyes. Her mum classed hard times as someone who couldn't buy the latest Jaguar.

'This is lovely, Barbara. Where is this from?' Reem ran her hand over the dresser that stood adjacent to the dining table. It was a burnt red, mahogany. The inlay details were in a geometric pattern she had seen before. Tiny mosaics, formed together, glued into place to form an intricate pattern that danced around the edges.

'We bought that off our good pal, Steven.'

'Is this from the Middle East?'

'Gosh no, it's hard enough getting furniture delivered from Hackney,' Barbara laughed. 'Leah, you remember Jonathan?' she said, opening the kitchen door.

Leah noticed her mother's pitch turn higher than usual. It always happened when she did something she knew Leah wouldn't like and this was no different. Of course she remembered Jonathan. Leah knew they wanted her to choose him instead of Matthew, and she couldn't believe her mum had the audacity to invite him. Jonathan stood at the door frame, his hands tucked into pockets with that same over-confident smile spread across his cheeks and his hair swept up, blow dried into place in a darker blonde than it was naturally.

'I haven't seen you in ages, Leah. Where have you been hiding?' Jonathan said, waltzing over and planting two wet kisses on her cheeks.

Leah winced and looked at Reem.

Reem smiled awkwardly. 'Leah, didn't you want to show me the gardens?'

'Yes, I did. Excuse us.'

Outside, the garden was lit with tiers of lights climbing up the different levels of flower beds and landscaping. Solar lights were planted in the soil beds, winding up to the back of the grass where a canopy and table sat at the far end of the garden.

'Thank you for that,' said Leah. 'My parents aren't always great at understanding what I want.'

'I am sure they are just trying to help.'

Leah never knew how to respond to Reem. Everything seemed so simple to her. Leah didn't know whether Reem was being sarcastic, but the way her eyes gazed into the distance and her hands ran gently along the flowers as she spoke made Leah realise it wasn't said with any bad intention. Nothing she said was. That was probably why Elijah liked her so much.

'He's not so bad, I guess. I'm just not ready to forget about Matthew.'

'What happened?'

'Heart failure. He died, a year and a half ago.'

'To God we belong and to God we return.'

'Yeah, I guess,' Leah said, not expecting the reply. Usually people would apologise but she never understood that either. It wasn't their fault. If anything, it was hers.

Elijah appeared behind them. 'Mummy, grandma said I can stay here tonight.'

'No, darling, you have to come home with me. Maybe next time.' Elijah bounded off back into the house.

A piercing screech split through the sky. Reem ran and ducked under the table. Her eyes shut. Her memory flashed back to a noise the same as that one, on a night back home that she couldn't piece together. It was followed by explosions and drops of light fizzling in the sky. Leah ran over. 'Reem, don't worry. It's just fireworks.'

Leah watched Reem look up at the sky. Catherine wheels in illuminous blue and rockets whizzing up in white streams battered against the sky until cheers came from the neighbours next door.

'They're having a party next door.'

'Dinner is ready!' Leah's dad shouted out into the garden.

Leah linked her arm with Reem's, concerned that she wasn't speaking. Her frame was withered under the attack and her eyes were distant as though she had revisited somewhere she hadn't wanted to go.

Dusk had fallen and although the others didn't notice, Leah heard Reem whisper something in Arabic before eating. She must have been breaking her fast, she thought. She looked at the quiet table, the clinking of silver knives and forks on the Wedgewood plates, the intimate conversations about work and the weather, and Leah thought how much nicer it would be if they were back on the patch of grass near home, under the open sky, eating from paper plates.

Chapter 12

~ Reem ~

The thought of returning home now filled Reem with dread. It was as though her life had been transported and placed in someone else's. She had barely known Nazim back in Syria and she didn't like the reminders he brought with him. The colours of her hometown seemed duller, muted. Without him, she could cling onto memories that were good, of when she was young. When Mahmoud was there. When food was in abundance. And since she moved, she was enjoying her English classes and sitting with Laila. Spending time with Leah and Elijah. Sometimes they would come over, but she had been making excuses not to see them since Nazim had arrived. Elijah had caught sight of him on one of his visits, and it hurt Reem to turn him away but he was old for his years. He understood. She didn't want Nazim around Elijah. He had a bad reputation back home. He was a pawnbroker, one of the only ones to get rich whilst everyone else was falling into poverty. He would trade whatever he could, whatever was going at the highest price. And that was when Reem's mother mentioned him in the house. It was when the war was getting bad and most people had begun to leave, their options running out.

Reem remembered that day. How she had cried and said she would rather stay at home, but then Adar would have also been kept behind. Nazim arranged for him to go as part of the wedding deal. That was the first concession of her adult life. He arranged for the journey out of Syria. The rest was a blur. The memories didn't even try to break through. There were none that Reem wanted to remember except the handful she repeated to herself, so they wouldn't fade and be lost with time.

At least here in a new country she could shed what was left behind. She had a chance at a new start. She had physically escaped but with him nearby, the streets of Syria leaked into London. The fear swept through the streets, the anxiety followed her in shadows that lurked around corners. It crept into places and watched her from the skies, waiting to fall on her with full force. It was a feeling she couldn't shake.

She opened the door and found Nazim inside. The place had changed. Black gowns were hanging on the curtain rails, there was a pile of paperwork on the table, his clothes were strewn on the backs of the sofa and two suitcases were open wide and half-packed in the centre of the lounge. She stood in the doorway.

'Well, come in then,' Nazim said, unusually upbeat.

'I can't stay long. My lesson is soon. *Shoofi*? What's all this?' Reem asked, walking over to the curtain in a home that no longer felt like hers. She stroked the black fabric of the dresses. 'Are you going somewhere?'

'That's what I wanted to talk to you about. I've decided we're moving.'

'What?'

'We're moving. This place isn't good for you, just look at how you've changed. I barely recognise you in your tight trousers and lumpy cardigans.'

'I'm pregnant, Nazim. Everything's tight – I –'

'Shush, shush. Don't worry about that. I bought these for you,' he said, looking pleased with himself as he unhooked a black gown from the curtain rail. 'I found them in the *souk*. They look just like the *abayas* back home,' he said, handing one to her.

Reem placed it in her lap. She didn't think they looked like the beautiful gowns back home. The fabric was cheap and she could feel it scratching between her fingertips.

'Well, aren't you going to say thank you?' His voice changed and his breathing was suddenly heavier.

'Yes, yes. *Shukran*.'

'Don't just stare at it. Put it on.'

'I'll do it later. I don't really wear them here –'

'Put. It. On.' Nazim was standing so close to her that she could smell the alcohol on his breath. She took off her cardigan and slipped it over her clothes. It was so loose that it would still cover her stomach even with clothes underneath.

'And the rest.' Nazim gestured to the black face veil that tied around the back of her headscarf. 'There – that's what a wife of mine should wear. I bought you enough so you don't have to wear these other clothes. And you can stop going to those English classes. It isn't fit for you to be out gallivanting every day, leaving your husband at home unattended.'

'It's good for work, Nazim. Think of the money I could earn when I can get a better job. It will be good for us both,' she said, desperately trying to cling to the freedom slipping away from her.

'None of that will matter in Jordan. I've booked the tickets. We leave in a few days.'

Reem paused, her mind working furiously to try and think of an answer to both appease him and get her out of it. 'I'm pregnant. They won't let me fly so close to the due date.'

'They'll never be able to see in these,' he said, yanking another *abaya* down and putting it in the suitcase.

'It's dangerous, for me and the baby. I...'

'Don't tell me what's good for my child. As for you, nothing but a mule for my son.' He had his hands gripped around her arm, pressing his fingers into her skin.

'What about Adar?' Reem said, her eyes watering from the pain simultaneously pulsating in her arm and chest.

'It is a shame what happened, but you've given it enough time. I won't let you use him as an excuse anymore.'

Reem was sweating underneath the black fabric. She tugged it off and slipped out of the dress, folding it over the back of the sofa, her hands shaking.

'Put it in the suitcase,' Nazim ordered.

'Please, Nazim. I'll do anything, don't make me go,' Reem said, grasping his hands. 'Please.'

'Don't beg, Reem. It doesn't suit you.'

'But why do we have to go? We can make it work here.'

'It isn't about us, you stupid girl. You don't understand anything.' Nazim grabbed a bottle and gulped the brown liquid down. 'I owe them money.'

'Who?'

'Stop asking so many questions,' he said, staggering backwards. He grabbed at the curtains as he fell backwards, tipping the bottle over his face and gasping for air.

'Now look what you made me do!' he yelled, lurching forward but just missing Reem. 'Now get out, before you make me do something I regret! This is your fault. Get out! And tell them you won't be coming back!' he shouted, as she darted for the door.

She arrived at her English class stumbling over the shoes that she had quickly pressed her feet into and broken the backs down in haste. Laila immediately sensed something was up. Reem told her she was flustered because her husband had turned up unexpectedly. Laila seemed pleased, until she saw Reem's face.

'At least it will be more helpful with the baby coming,' Laila said.

The sentence came to her like a blow. Reem couldn't concentrate on the lesson and she went outside to sit on the steps overlooking the quiet side road. She heard a familiar voice coming from the other side of the hall. The men's section.

'I hadn't considered marriage, but I feel it is the right thing to do.'

It was Mo. Reem knew she shouldn't be listening but she couldn't help overhearing him. 'We should be helping our sisters. And if I can do it, then there is goodness in it?'

'Yes, much goodness, brother. But you need to be ready for marriage. It's half your religion. You must be sure.' Reem was sure this was the *imam* speaking.

'I don't have much time left to decide. She's on a list and deportation procedures could start in a few months.'

'Then pray two *rakah* and ask Allah to help you to make your decision.'

Laila came out and joined Reem. 'Are you okay, *habibte*? You don't seem yourself today?' She held Reem's arm.

Reem winced and pulled down her sleeve to cover the bruise underneath, but judging by Laila's face, she had already seen it.

'You missed the lesson,' Laila said.

'It doesn't matter. I won't be coming anymore.'

'Why not?'

'I'm leaving, Laila. He wants to move to Jordan. He says he has work there, that it's better for us,' Reem said, trying to unfold the backs of her shoes and fit her feet into them properly.

'When?'

'He's already booked the tickets. We leave in a few days.'

Laila sat down on the edge of the steps. 'But you can't fly. You are about to give birth any day!'

'He said I can hide it under my *abaya* and they'll never know.'

'But what if –' Laila began.

Reem shrugged her shoulders, anticipating that whatever Laila said next wouldn't matter. None of it mattered.

'I'll be sad to see you leave,' Laila said, staring at the same spot on the ground as she spoke.

Reem didn't want to answer and didn't need to as Mo walked out of the mosque at that moment.

Laila stood up quickly. '*Salam* Mo.'

'Wa alaikom salam,' he replied, not making eye contact with either of them. He rushed off ahead.

'I didn't know you knew Mo?' Reem asked.

'I don't know him that well, really. We were involved in some community stuff together a while back and he helped me with organising that.'

Reem nodded, but she was barely concentrating.

'Are you okay to go home tonight?' Laila asked. 'I have a small apartment. Well, tiny actually, but you are welcome.'

Reem looked at the tower. The lights were on in some of the windows. Behind the glass, obscure figures moved. Reem wanted so much to go, to run miles away from the building, away from Nazim. But she couldn't involve Laila. If Nazim came looking for her and found Laila there too, there would be no telling what he would do and Reem couldn't live with herself if she dragged Laila into it.

'Thank you, but I'm okay, really.'

Laila rubbed her shoulders. 'Okay, well, call me if you need me.'

Reem smiled and waved as she left. She went back into the mosque and read some Qur'an. She glanced at the clock. She had until the end of *taraweeh* prayer before the doors shut for the night, and until then to find somewhere else to go.

***

Reem clasped her hands over her stomach as a wave of intense pain rolled over her. Reem thought if she imagined hard enough that she wasn't pregnant, it would go away. Silently slip away in the night like an unwanted nightmare. This wasn't the life she had imagined for herself. The days when she used to stroll down the wide tree-lined streets and walk into the university hall, she had pictured herself as a lecturer, a scholar. She let out a laugh thinking about how stupid and naïve she had been. She didn't know then how life could turn.

Another wave of pain cramped her stomach from under her chest to where she felt the baby's hard bones jab into the flesh of her thighs as she crouched down. She left the mosque before the prayers had started so no one was there. Outside, the cool air slightly eased the heat pulsating through her forehead. She had been secretly watching films of mothers giving birth by themselves. She had read stories of them giving birth in aeroplane toilets, in cafes, in the back of taxis. She had it all planned out. She would go up to the apartment, fetch towels and hot water. A sharp pair of scissors. No one would have to know. She could decide what to do afterwards. No one would see her body, no one would have to know that she had given birth. That she had been a mother, even temporarily. After the war, she could pick up her life from where she had left it. She could go back to school, finish her masters. Make a difference. But with Nazim here, that was no longer an option.

Her legs felt heavy as she tried to move one foot in front of the other, but when the pain came she was paralysed. Helpless, she leaned against the wall of the tower, sandwiched between the shadows of the buildings surrounding her. She knew at that moment that she couldn't do this by herself. Her only alternative was to go to the hospital. In that moment the fear of becoming a mother, of having a baby to take care of, was replaced by a darker fear. This time it was recurring images that forced her to the ground. The smell of bleach. The glint of the scalpels. She would rather die in the shadows, her body intact. At least it was her own. Her nerves felt every shoot of pain because this is what she had done to herself. This is what she deserved.

The journey was almost automatic. She pressed the buzzer by the staff's night entrance and was relieved to see it was Archie who was on night security.

'You aren't on the rota for tonight?'

'No. I didn't have anywhere else to go,' Reem winced and kneeled down, her hand clasped to her stomach.

'Are you okay? What's wrong?'

'Nothing, I will be okay. I just need to sit down, I think.'

Archie helped her in and called Kesandu.

Kesandu came rushing over and took one look at Reem before saying, 'Thanks, Archie. I'll take it from here.'

Reem saw Archie watching them down the hall and she managed to throw him a smile and put her hand to her forehead. He did the same. He had told her how he was a boat captain back in St. Kitts, how he had left to come to the UK for a better life, but everyday he saved up to get back to his island to fish. He saved the money once, Kesandu had told her, but he came back after a few weeks. 'Home changes. When you leave and go back, it never feels the same again.'

Reem remembered her saying it because she hadn't believed it. But seeing Archie, towering above them in the corridor with a worried look in his eyes, Reem could never imagine him being a fisherman in the Caribbean Sea, with the sun beating down on his face. She couldn't imagine him wearing bright colours and making a living on a tropical sea, when the last three decades of his life had been spent living nocturnally underground, with his vision lit only by a torch.

Kesandu took Reem down into the laundry area of the hotel. It was empty, excluding the pyramids of unwashed laundry piled in the centre in soft trolleys.

'So, lady, you ready to tell me now?'

'What?' Reem said, through gasps of breath.

'That the baby you're expecting is about to meet us?'

Reem looked at her in surprise.

'Come on girl, I weren't born yesterday. Same thing happened to my cousin. She tried to hide it. She didn't have no baby daddy around, but I knew. I could tell straight away.' Kesandu smiled, like she was pleased she could see through people's secrets.

'Who else knows?'

'Mostly, er, everyone. Well, anyone who has seen you during the last few weeks.' Kesandu laughed.

Usually it was this bubbliness that Reem loved about Kesandu and it made coming to work easier, but right now it wasn't what she wanted. The pain shot through her stomach and wrapped around her back, making it impossible to breathe. Reem was sure this was a sign that she shouldn't have the baby. It was a foreboding, anxious feeling that she had tried to shake off since she found out. But then the weeks passed, her body changed and she felt movements flutter inside her. Like the tick-tocking of a clock, counting down to her life being altered. Her old life would well and truly be gone. Her dreams of finishing her studies, of returning to her mum and of those days with her brother, faded into the past. But that was long ago; the country was in ruins, the hotels abandoned, and as for her parents, she wasn't even sure if they were still alive.

And here she was, completely unprepared with no one around, soon to be in charge of a life she hadn't wanted, living with a man she saw no escape from. She screamed with the pain, the disappointment, the lack of control over her own body and feelings and dreams. And almost instantly, after the stabbing pain subsided, blood began streaming down her legs, staining the white sheets.

'Girl, I'm calling you an ambulance.'

'No, you can't. Please.'

'I don't have a choice.'

Kesandu walked off to call the ambulance, leaving Reem alone on the pile of sheets. Reem could make out parts of the phone call. Labour. Emergency. She's bleeding.

But the pause was too long. It should have been over. Maybe because her husband wasn't here, they weren't going to come. She was going to be left by herself.

When Kesandu came back, the permanent smile that lit up her dimpled cheeks was gone. The colour had drained from her face.

'They aren't coming, are they?'

'They are going to try and send someone as soon as they can but...'

'But what?'

'There has been an accident back where you live. The building. It's on fire.'

~ Leah ~

Leah opened her eyes to thick, black smoke seeping in through the doors, up through the cracks in the floorboards. She scrambled out of bed and crawled on the floor as the smoke billowed above her head. The layout of her once familiar apartment shifted into a disconnected puzzle. She was supposed to be at Elijah's bedroom door but instead she hit into walls that shouldn't have been there, knocked against something that must have been the coffee table in the lounge.

Barely able to breathe, she turned around and stumbled back towards where she thought his room was. She felt around the door frame searching for the handle, but the door was already wide open. She called out to him. She wasn't sure if what she was saying came out or if it was in her mind, desperately trying to find its way out through her lips. She felt around his blankets, his sheets, trying to find his little body amidst the quilts. She couldn't feel him. Panic slapped her across the chest and a choking feeling gripped her neck.

The thick swell of poisonous smoke now filling the apartment, she lost her bearings. A crack of light came from the front door. It was ajar. A moment of clarity; the fire hadn't yet reached the stairwell. It was coming up through the floorboards, near the north window frames. Her front door was open. She stumbled towards it, unsure of what lay on the other side.

The building creaked and moaned. Debris rained from the ceilings. The smell of burning plastic was toxic in the air and dripped from the ceilings. She could hear her heart beating as though it was outside her body. But she couldn't be sure if it was her heartbeat as she saw bodies moving through the corridors. She heard coughing, screams in the distance, panicked footsteps. There was no rhythm – just chaos. She looked down the stairwell. Some ran upstairs. Disorientated in the smoke. Some ran downstairs, pushing past one another. Holding babies. Children crying as they were yanked down the centre stairwells. Was Elijah one of them? She was sure she shouted for him but she couldn't make out any of the figures that walked like him. None were his size. His small frame. A nine-year-old lost amidst the storm of ash coating the floors, the stairs, the walls. Encroaching on their city as it was being buried under the ash.

What if he had gone to the garden or he was one of those bodies running upstairs to the roof? She ran up the stairwell with an energy given to her by the adrenaline coursing through her blood. Her mind was racing now. She was sure if she couldn't see him down the stairwell then he might have followed the people who had gone upstairs. It made sense. In the films he watched, people went to the roof. The garden. It was a sanctuary of fresh air amidst the smoke. What if he had gone to save the bees or to save his seedlings? The garden was on the opposite side to the fire. Maybe it hadn't spread there yet. He was only nine. He wouldn't be thinking clearly. Leah managed the first three flights with surprising ease and pushed the door out onto the courtyard. In the space, in the darkness, she could see the shadows of empty chairs. The silhouettes of plants. She could hear the hum of the bees. The stillness felt eerie. The moon was a sharp slice in the blackness of the sky. She ran over to the railings, taking in mouthfuls of air, refuelling her lungs with oxygen. 'Elijah!' she called. She darted to where he had begun his Middle Eastern garden. The small seed pot remained undisturbed. He hadn't been there. Leah peered over the edge. An emergency response team had pulled in front of the building. Fire engines, ambulances and police cars washed the lower part of the building with red and blue light.

She had to leave. She had to find Elijah. She ran inside, taken aback by how quickly the smoke had thickened. She grappled at railings and spiralled down the stairs. A floor down, she stopped, leaning against a door. It opened. A figure dressed in bedclothes looked at her through grey eyes and went to shut the door.

'You have to leave. The building is on fire.' Leah was sure she was saying it clearly so she was shocked that the elderly woman didn't move.

'They told us to stay. They told us to stay,' she said instead, shaking her wiry grey hair with the force of her resistance.

'You have to leave,' Leah pleaded.

'I can hear them, listen.' The elderly woman paused.

Leah stopped.

In the faint distance, she heard the whirr of sirens. They sounded like they belonged somewhere else. Leah grabbed her arm. Shocked, she pushed Leah away and slammed the door. Leah heard the lock bolt shut with a resounding clang. She turned to leave, to find the stairwell, to carry on down towards the air, but the smoke had become too thick. She tripped and fell. Someone had left something in the stairwell. She kneeled down, her hands running over it expecting to remove a bike or a chunk of the crumbling building, but it was softer. It felt fleshy under her finger-tips. Damp, hot. In a flash of the emergency light, under its green warning, she saw it was a body. Instinctively, she grabbed and tried to pull and pull and pull. But she barely moved.

'Please, get up. We have to leave.'

Leah wasn't sure if she was even talking now, or if, like in a nightmare, she had no voice. No sound left her lips despite wanting to scream at the top of her lungs. She realised that underneath the woman's body was a child with soft hair, untouched by the ash, shielded by her mother, lying motionless on the ground floor. For a moment, despite the consuming atmosphere and smothering blankets of smoke layering the air, she saw the girl's face with such clarity that she couldn't move. Perfectly made lips, pressed closed. A delicate nose frozen in time, unmoving, unbreathing. Her skin, honeyed and bright, free from ash, kept pure under her mother's top. She looked like a snow angel, cutting out a shape in the blackness. If she had any moisture left in her body, she would have cried but her throat felt burnt. Her eyes were stinging, and she could barely see. Her body felt bereft of any energy. She knelt down and began crawling towards the door. These were her last moments and all she saw was the girl's face and Elijah's. The two images flashed in her mind like a black and white film. There was no sound. A sign in front of her noted she was on the third floor. It hit her like a dead weight in the chest. She had thought she was almost out. She was alone now. There was no one else there. She dragged herself down to the second. But by then, she could barely see. She hit into soft lumps on the floor. Clambering over them, she counted without meaning to. One, two, three, four...

Hazy vision. No sound. Breathing burnt her lungs. She was slumped by Elijah's bed. Her mind imagined him coming to her. His hands open. She held her hand out in front of her. Her eyes opened. But it was not Elijah she saw. A face she vaguely recognised moved through the smoke. A flash of white. A brief wisp of musk. Rougher skin touching her hand, pulling her to her feet. Lifting her. Suddenly, her body was motionless. She rested, her head lolling behind. As she was being carried out, her eyes glanced at the floor. Shapes of those who hadn't made it cut through the ash on the floor as it sprinkled down, burying them underneath the blackness. So close, she thought. Inches away from the door, their hands outstretched towards the light.

She was carried in the rhythm of someone else's heavy footsteps. Methodical, rushed. She smelt something familiar and heady on her skin. 'Take her,' he said gently, handing her over to a paramedic, his uniform stained with black smears and blood. His unfamiliar voice asked who she was.

'I'm Elijah's mother.'

Her body slumped by the ambulance doors as he placed an oxygen mask around her face, checked her pulse. She sat there, unable to move, just staring at the scene around her. She saw the back of her rescuer. He moved quickly. He headed straight back through the doors, his white, stained clothes vanishing into the mouth of the hallway. He was wearing white. It had been white before. There was something about his movements. Something she recognised and found familiar, but she couldn't work out what it was. When he re-emerged he was barely recognisable. He dragged someone out and went to dart back in, but a uniformed policeman grabbed him. He struggled and pushed, until the entrance way almost gave in. Another man ran out, coughing and spluttering. Their faces black from the fire. He took him and headed to the ambulances on the far side of the building, before they were sped off down the street.

The flames roared into the black sky, dwarfing out the thin slice of moon. The windows and the whole north side were engulfed in leaping flames. Firefighters aimed hoses at the lower floors but the water wasn't enough to quell the flames. Smouldering, burning lumps of the building fell off in blocks, falling to the ground. Leah's eyes looked up and followed the fire.

'I need to get inside, I have to help. My son is in there.'

The paramedic darted off to the firefighting team. Her heart raced. Her head felt dizzy and she tried to stand up, to move towards them. To get inside, to do something. She couldn't just stay there. She tried to stand on her feet, but the weight of her standing caused her legs to cave in. Unable to even move, all she could do was watch in utter horror as they were lost behind a screen of fire. She fell to the floor, coughing. She couldn't catch her breath. She coughed up black blood, choking her lungs. The night time air filled her with more blackness. She couldn't taste the fresh air. She fell to the floor. She was back with the bodies in the building, spinning in the darkness, trying to find a way to escape but she couldn't. Was Elijah there? Unable to breathe, terrified without her. Her worst nightmares danced in the smoke. They shifted into the figure of him. Floating away, drifting into the abyss. She tried with everything she had left to try and pull him back to her, but the expanse was too immense.

In a dreamlike, surreal state, she glanced up to the sky. And just then, even though afterwards it would seem absurd, she saw the bees. Just glimpses of them. Hovering, swarming above the building before they too were lost in the flames. Her eyes adjusted. She looked around her to get space, to get proportion. The figures on the garden courtyard morphed. Leah's heart sank. They were not the bees. They were the frantic, waving arms of those yet to be saved.

***

Leah opened her eyes. She felt tubes inside her nose and the entry point to a drip bruising her arm. A swift moment of relief gave way to an overwhelmingly sickening feeling. She swung her head over the side of the bed and threw up. A nurse rushed in and called to some other staff.

'My name is Martisha. I am your nurse...' She paused, studying Leah's face. 'I recognise you?'

'Where is Elijah? My son. Please, you have to find him. I –'

'Okay, let me get someone dealing with the crisis.'

'What happened?'

Martisha shoved Leah's legs up to plant her heavy behind on the edge of the bed as her white uniform tightened around the bulges in her middle.

'There was a fire in your apartment building.'

She spoke in a tone Leah had heard on the wards before to shocked patients. Leah sat back, stunned. She imagined the outside of the building, the fire raging into the night sky as she was being loaded into the ambulance. Screams of fear rang from the windows. Amidst the chaos there was a little boy she had to protect. She swung her legs out of the bed and pulled the drip from her arm. Her legs felt unsteady beneath her. She pulled back the curtain.

Stretchers were being wheeled in. She didn't recognise the charred skin of people, their mouths covered with oxygen masks. The chaos of Accident & Emergency in a crisis. The beds were full, people were laying the corridor. She heard crying, yelps of pain. A voice. A sob. A child's. She scoured around and saw the back of a boy hunched over by a bed.

She ran over to him. 'Elijah!' He turned around. She took two steps back as she registered his face. Scorched on one side by the fire. It wasn't Elijah. He pointed up at the patient in the bed. Automatically, she pressed her fingers into his pulse and placed her face near his mouth. 'Medic, we need a resuscitation kit.'

A nurse wheeled one over to her. There was no one free. 'I need a doctor over here.'

A man in doctor's scrubs ran over and wiped the brow of his forehead. His face creased. Tired. He looked at her and then stopped to look again. 'Leah?'

'Dr Sameer.' Leah handed him the kit. 'Take over, I need to find Elijah.'

Martisha ran towards her. 'You shouldn't be out of bed. Come on.'

'I've already told you, I need to find my son. He is only nine. He will be scared... he... he doesn't know where I am.'

'The police are here. They have a team to help.'

Leah paused. Her feet didn't move. 'Please, if you just come back to bed. I will send him to you now.' Martisha paused and furrowed her brow. 'The police officer won't be able to find you if you're roaming about the hospital.'

Leah went back to her bed. Her knee knocked up and down as she chewed the edges of her nails. She saw the TV in the corner of the room. A murky black sky lit up by the fire raging through the tower block. Keeping her curtains open, she avoided looking at the screen and instead scanned everybody who walked through the doors, praying that Elijah would be one of them. She could imagine him, walking in with his jet plane. He would see her and run to her. 'Mummy, I've found you!' he might shout in excitement and she would feel silly for being so worried.

'Mrs Streatfield?' The police officer hunched up his trousers at the knees and sat in the chair next to her bed. 'Do you mind?' he said, gesturing to his hat.

'Please help me. My son. He was in there,' Leah said, gesturing to the TV, her index finger shaking uncontrollably as she pointed. 'He is nine years old, his name is Elijah. Brown hair. Curly. Long. He liked to tuck it behind his ears. He is wearing his dinosaur pyjamas –'

'What is your apartment number?'

'608.'

He stopped writing and glanced up at her, yanking out his collar and loosening the top button.

'Tell me, what is it?'

'The fire. It started on the fifth floor. Right underneath your apartment.'

~ Reem ~

'What are we going to do?'

'There isn't much we can do, just stay calm.'

'What do you mean, stay calm? I am about to have a baby in the laundry room.'

'It could be worse. At least we have plenty of towels,' Kesandu said. Reem saw she was smiling but underneath, a ripple of panic stirred.

'Just take deep breaths and when your body tells you to push, you push, okay?'

'No, no I don't want to. I can't have a baby.'

'Well that baby is coming, ain't nothing you can do about it.'

Reem slowed her breathing down and tried to take in deep breaths as sweat ran down her forehead. Waves of contractions rolled in and became so painful that she was sure she was going to pass out. She laid back on the heap of soft sheets, wondering how she ended up being one of those people giving birth in secret, underground in a hotel she worked in.

'Push!' Kesandu squealed, almost with excitement. 'I can see something.'

Reem tucked her head into her chest and closed her eyes, imagining she was at home under the cool, fresh air of the pomegranate tree. But it kept mixing with the smell of blood and formaldehyde. Images flashed of a ring on the surgeon's hand. His name was called out but she couldn't recall what it was. The pain flooded back, her eyes opened. She screamed and pushed, but the baby wasn't out.

'Come on, Reem. You have to push harder.'

'Where is the ambulance? I can't do it.'

'You have to. This isn't the Reem I know. The Reem I know is tough.'

Reem focused through the intense burning pain. '*Ya Allah*, save us!' and pushed one last time, feeling the solid body of the baby leave hers and enter the world, bloodying the white sheets she was lying on.

Reem looked at her. She was the most beautiful girl she had ever seen. Kesandu wrapped the sheets around the newborn and darted off. Archie had arrived at the laundry room doors with the paramedics.

'Wait,' said Reem, as they carted her off on a stretcher. The paramedics stopped. Reem clutched Kesandu's hand, tears streamed down both of their faces. 'How can I ever repay you for this?'

'Pray for me,' Kesandu said, blowing her a kiss.

Reem waved at her even after the doors had shut. She could see her through the window. Her face, so familiar now and always to be a part of her future. She knew she was emotional but it wasn't just the birth, or the baby. It was also Kesandu. The kindness of strangers, the people she didn't know she needed in her life that were given to her with Allah's perfect timing. She cried because between all the evil, there were rays of hope. Inara, she thought, ray of light. She would name her daughter Inara as a reminder to never give up hope.

The ambulance pulled off and Reem couldn't see the outside. But she heard it. She heard the wails of sirens, police fire engines, more ambulances. She heard shouting, screaming, strained panic in voices. She closed her eyes and even imagined that she could hear the flames roaring as they tore through the building. She didn't want to think of it anymore, her nerves suspended, tightly strung. It couldn't be her building. Kesandu must have been mistaken. But when she arrived at the hospital, the TV screens confirmed that it was. The night sky was alight as the fire raged, the flames covering half of the building. It was blazing up the sides of the buildings, the windows were blocked and Reem thought she could see bodies falling from them.

Her hands were shaking as she dialled everyone she knew. No one answered.

~ *Leah* ~

'Leah, can I talk to you?'

'Mo, is that you?' Leah answered as he walked in through the curtain. 'Oh my goodness, look at your hands, your face.'

'They're burnt but *alhamdulilah* I am alive.'

'Were you in the apartment when it happened?'

'No. I was at the night prayers with Nidal. They're longer in Ramadan so we were awake. When we came home, the building was already on fire.'

'How did you get burnt then?'

'We ran in. We had to get as many people out as possible.'

Leah clasped her hand over her mouth. She lay back in the bed. She was carried out, she saw a flash of his white robe, his familiar voice in her ear. She took a few moments to reacquaint herself. The images were blurry. She knew Elijah wasn't there.

'You did it? You saved me?'

Mo nodded, but there was something he was holding back. 'I tried, Leah.'

'What do you mean?'

Mo paused, allowing Leah to form the thoughts for herself. Elijah. She looked at Mo.

'Elijah?'

'I carried him first. I got to his room, I rushed him out. Leah, the paramedics saw to him straight away. He was one of the first but –'

'No. Please.'

'He didn't make it, Leah. I am so sorry.'

~ *Reem* ~

Reem heard Leah scream from behind the curtain. She wanted to go in, but she didn't dare. The scream curdled her blood, and she realised it must have been about Elijah. The only sound it could have been was the pain of a mother losing her child. From behind a curtain, she watched Mo walk out, crying. He pushed Nidal away and left the ward, the crowded hallways, the stretchers and beds filled with the victims, the survivors of the fire.

Reem couldn't bring herself to see Leah, Mo or Nidal. Everyone had lost people in the fire. She felt guilty for not being there, for feeling the love she had for her newborn baby. She went back up to the maternity ward, barely breathing in case someone recognised her and she would have to show them that she and the baby were okay.

Suddenly, she remembered Nazim. She couldn't settle. She roamed the corridors looking into people's faces, trying to see if she could find him, but he wasn't there. Reem couldn't rest. She hated every second of being in hospital. The sounds, the smells, all of it made her nauseous. The hospital had descended into chaos. The rooms were filling up and patients were put on other wards. Reem held her baby close, hobbling around, sure she would hear Nazim's voice behind her. Surprising her, terrifying her. Taking her baby. Taking her.

She panicked so much she could barely breathe. The thick, warm air of the wards and the smell of ash, smoke and medicine mingled together, making her feel sick. She wrapped the baby to her chest and walked out of the hospital.

She walked down the streets, her clothes stained, her body feeling like it was falling apart underneath her, but she was free at least. Inara was warm against her, content. Safe. Reem hopped onto a bus and stared out of the window as it pulled her closer towards the fire. Orange flames flickered into the night sky. Fire engines, ambulances and police cars surrounded the building. Reem could still see people inside. She joined the crowd outside. Amidst all the horror, they stood silently staring, unable to help as the fire raged through the building and silhouettes appeared behind the windows. Reem looked up to the floor where she used to live. Her belongings burnt away, the pieces she stole now turned to ash. Nazim. If he was inside, he would not have survived. He couldn't have survived this. The floors surrounding her apartment were engulfed.

Reem stood behind the police tape, watching as the firemen trudged in and out. Inara was wrapped closely underneath her clothes. She couldn't return home, so she wasn't sure where she should be. It was almost instinctive that she should be there, waiting to go back inside, even though looking at the building she knew that was impossible. No one would return there. She waited to see if Nazim would come out and she imagined him walking towards her, almost untouched by the smoke. But no one walked out except for the firemen, carrying zipped black bags away from the scene. Reem noticed how the emergency services were parked, how they orchestrated who was to do what and when. There wasn't the panic and disorder like there had been back home. In her country, the scenes of accidents meant a heightened threat. Bombs were detonated for maximum casualties when the crowd drew close. But at least back home the people were allowed to help. Not like here. Here they were kept back, roped off from going any further. It was a physical distance Reem hadn't experienced before. There, the emergency area was hard to distinguish since almost everywhere looked like a war zone, against a backdrop of already broken pavement slabs and shop windows and bent metal. The locals would be pulling people out, administering first aid whilst the ambulances, struggling with staff and funds, took too long to reach them.

Her mind felt numb, but the creeping feeling wormed its way in. She moved past people whose faces were awash with fear. She could almost hear the suspension of their breathing as all their eyes stared in the same direction. Their lips moving with prayers, with names, with a hope left that their loved ones were already safe. Under the cloak of darkness, it seemed unreal that it was near.

Slowly, people in reflective jackets came, holding clipboards. They moved through the crowds of people, taking names. Directing people to different areas. Reem. Resident. Nazim was staying with her. Six foot tall. Fifth floor. Apartment number 517. Community centre. They listened, following orders, moving in an orderly way, clearing the area. Waiting on the news of those who were left behind.

Inside the community centre, temporary accommodation had been set up. Food was being brought in and placed on tables. Blankets were being piled up inside, reminding Reem of where she had been placed when she first arrived. When she allowed herself to sit down, she slumped against the wall, realising how exhausted she was. Inara finished feeding and fell asleep, pressed against Reem's chest. Reem thought how Inara saw nothing else in the room except her. How in Inara's world, everything was pure and untouched. But for Reem, it was too late. In her head, she saw flashes of nightmares that flickered between the fire, hospital and home.

Reem awoke to the sound of sobs, coughing, babies crying and children asking for food. She fed Inara and sat up bleary-eyed to see families asleep on the floor together. Others were going to serve breakfast from the table set up in the corner. The cleanly dressed ones must have been the ones organising what happened next, the government workers who were confirming names and trying to set up temporary accommodation. Myriam and Ayesha came over to her. She was in a daze, she didn't understand everything they were saying. Reem was assessed. They asked for the baby's name and birth date and when she told them, an ambulance was called to take Reem back to the hospital.

'I didn't want to go, we are fine. Please don't send us there.'

Reem was to be taken into emergency accommodation. They walked her past the crowds to a lower rise building, only fifteen or so storeys that made up part of their community. In the centre of it was the smouldering tower. She would have the health visitor and her social worker informed.

'Take it, before they all go.'

Reem stared up at the building. She couldn't say anything else. She had to get inside and get Inara safe, despite it being so close that if she concentrated hard enough, she could see her old life turn to ashes in front of her, once again.

chapter 13

~ *Reem* ~

Everyone in the community had lost someone. Brianna lost Chantelle in the fire. Bill had died. The paintings he had left out to dry the night before were hung on the walls around the community centre. Harold had been awake, unable to sleep in the cleaning closet, and he went around the first few floors, battering on everyone's door and alerting them to the fire. The investigators said if it wasn't for the people returning from *taraweeh* prayers so late at night, many more would have perished. People were wearing 'Missing' T-shirts with the faces of their loved ones; others held vigils for those still missing. There were crowds of people around the building, memorials popping up by the Tube stations, donations littering the streets, but Reem, feeling guilty about her own arrival on everyone's night of terror, stayed by herself. She mourned his loss, his company, his stunted future, and was only resolved to be calmer when she reminded herself of the heaven above the skies that he would be at peace in.

It was only after a few weeks that she felt well enough to venture outside. Eid passed with no celebration. Her artefacts had gone except for the old coin still wrapped in newspaper in her pocket. The last link between her and her physical home. Reem remembered they hadn't been the only objects that reminded her of home. There had been one more. One more link between this island and her own. She decided she wanted to know the truth. If the fire had shown anything, it was how quickly life could be snatched away.

Unsure of how to get there, but now familiar with how to get across London, Reem looked at the Tube map and worked out that it would take about an hour to reach. She packed Inara's things and placed her in her stroller. She stopped at the first Tube station, walked to get on another line, and repeated that twice until she reached the borough of Hackney. It looked different to the usual spots she knew in London. Big art centres and warehouses backed onto unused patches of grass. She read the signs of the warehouses she passed but there was nothing that gave it away. It was a cold day and the rain drizzled relentlessly, creating pools of dirty water under the ridges of the pavements that wet her feet, as she aimlessly criss-crossed over the roads, searching for something that she didn't know how to find.

Tired, she sat down and fed Inara in a small corner café. She drank a strong coffee, and whilst gazing out of the window, preparing herself to leave, she heard someone behind her. It was an accent she knew. It sounded close to the Arabic spoken in her hometown.

At the table behind her, a few men sat down, wearing stained overalls and talking about how they were going to spend the weekend. She had no idea where else to look, so when they had finished lunch she followed them out onto the street. She stayed a decent distance behind them, not wanting to appear odd considering she was following strangers, but they didn't go far until they disappeared into a battered-looking warehouse that stood by itself, set back from the streets.

She knew she couldn't just go and knock on the door and she looked totally out of place, but she had come all this way and had to see what was inside. If this was the place. She walked over and banged on the door. Nothing. She banged again, and one of the younger men who was at the café opened the door slightly.

'Yes?'

'I am looking for Syrian furniture and antiquities,' Reem answered in English.

He looked at her, puzzled, so she switched to Arabic and repeated herself.

'You have to call the office,' he replied.

'Please can I come in, just for a second.'

'No, no way. You have a baby. Too dangerous.'

Reem stuck her foot in the door and tried to look over him.

'I just wanted to see how it's made. If it comes from here?'

'Please, you have to go.'

The man shut the door and Reem stood there for a few moments, wondering what she had expected to happen. She pushed Inara all the way to the Tube station, thankful that at least she was sleeping peacefully, despite the grey rain and disappointment.

'Excuse me,' said a voice behind her.

She stopped without turning around. The voice changed to Arabic.

'Do I know you?'

She knew the voice, but she couldn't place it. She had met so many people since she arrived that it was impossible to tell who it was. But somewhere in the back of her brain, it unlocked an opening, one that transported her back home, to the city streets, to the nights spent under the moonlit sky. She turned around. Standing on a colourless pavement, miles from home, he stood. Thinner than she remembered, more unkempt, his hair falling in front of his eyes, his hands sheepishly hidden his pockets. His threadbare clothes making him look cold in the overcast sunlight. There, on the same London street as her, was Mahmoud. Alive.

Reem couldn't move. The boy she'd known her whole life, the one she had lost and mourned so many times over could not possibly be standing on the street a few metres away from her. She looked at his face from the distance. She closed her eyes, allowing the rain to fall over her eyelids and soak her through, to bring back some feeling to her body as this moment seemed like a dream. Her memories took her right back to his family gardens in Syria. The grass was lush and green like it used to be. The old fruit trees were sturdy and firm, bearing ripe figs and pomegranates. Mahmoud was running between them, calling her to him as he hid behind their aged trunks. The sunlight dappled as it broke through the leaves lighting up the orchard floor as though it was their secret world to explore. She caught up with him and sought shade under the oldest tree as she watched him clamber up and pull down some figs for her to eat. He placed them in her open hands, baring his scratched-up fingers and bleeding knees splintered with wood. She looked back to the man standing in the rain. His hands were larger and still bore cuts. His legs didn't look strong enough to climb a tree. He stood there. His hands in his pockets, unlike the boy who had been in the orchard. The dark clouds rolled in, blocking out the sunlight. His face reflected not his boyhood, but his life ever since. Reem realised her memories were too old. The orchard had been burnt down. The trees were nothing but stumps of blackened ash. Stunted. As he walked towards her, she saw the scarring down his arms and hands. The ripples of once burnt skin running from his hands and disappearing under the sleeves of his shirt. She reached out and touched them. She saw him, not as he was then, but as the boy she pulled from the burning orchard as he desperately tried to extinguish the flames with the stale buckets of water that were left propped up against the trees and the hose that had long since run dry. Reem remembered she had sat with him, washing his charred skin as he sat there weeping quietly for a life that would never be restored. For fruit that would never regrow. For a war that stole everything they had ever loved. All Reem could do was concentrate on his arms. Methodically wrapping them with her torn headscarf pieces, praying that Allah would find them a way out. Reem's eyes welled as she realised how many times Allah had shown her a way out of things that seemed impossible. From back then in the orchard, to now.

She looked up at him. Her fingers recognising the grooves of his hands as he let her take it in. As slowly as she needed to. After all, after everything that happened, was she sure that this was happening? Could Mahmoud really be brought back to her over all the space between them? Through years of time and across oceans to a London street where they stood opposite each other, hand in hand? As the rain cleared and sunlight broke through, Reem's confidence was restored. He was there, breathing and alive. In the flesh. She didn't want to let him go again.

'Come and sit with me.'

'I would love to but –'

'Please don't tell me no. Not today, not when I've found you again after all this time.'

'I have to go back to work...' Mahmoud said, looking at his watch and glancing back at the warehouse.

'I won't keep you long. Just give me some time with you, to let this sink in so I know it's real,' Reem said, squeezing his hands tightly.

'You know I've never been able to say no to you,' Mahmoud said, gently knocking Reem on her arm with his hand and smiling.

He was as surprised as she was, she could tell, but he said that he had recognised her voice although it took him a while to work out who it belonged to. They sat in the same café she had been in before, and he told her about what had happened after his father died. How he defected from the army because he refused to kill his fellow countrymen and how he fled the country before he was tried for treason. He had been in Europe originally, but then he heard about an Englishman based in London who was looking for someone to head up the handmade furniture workshop he had. Mahmoud met with him and explained how he was trained in it, so, being promised a decent salary and accommodation, he took it. He had been working there for the last two years and although it wasn't what he expected, he was in a better situation than most people he knew.

Reem didn't say much, she was just pleased to see him. She couldn't help but worry about how different he looked, how worn and tired. But then she looked at her reflection in the café window. She didn't look anything like the girl he had known. And he was no longer the same boy.

'I have to go now. I have to get back to work but I want to see you again. Are you staying around here?'

'No, it's about an hour from here. I just moved, after the fire.'

'I heard about it. Everyone has, it's just... there aren't words.'

'People I knew died there. A young boy.' Reem looked away to take a deep breath. She thought of Elijah and tried to stop her tears. 'He was only nine.'

'Not Adar?'

'No, no. I haven't seen him since I arrived. The truth is, I can't remember –'

She looked down at Inara. Who would she become? Reem didn't want to think about it. She wasn't ready.

'That's happened to a few people I know, forgetting things, after trauma –' Mahmoud extended his hand to hers on the table and Reem pulled away.

'No, it isn't that. I must find him. His name is on an official list now, so it won't be long.' Mahmoud sat back in his chair. 'Nazim died there.'

Mahmoud didn't say a word. Reem knew he wouldn't speak ill of a dead person, no matter what Mahmoud thought of him when he was growing up. She had always admired how he stuck to what he believed was right. She used to think she was strong and that she knew her mind but everything that had happened had thrown her off course.

'And what about your dreams of preserving Syrian history?' Mahmoud said, changing the subject. 'That's probably impossible since the war. UNESCO heritage sites have been turned into rubble.'

Reem shifted in her chair and didn't look at him.

'Well, it's not like I could have done anything about that.'

'No, I'm sorry, that isn't what I meant. I –'

'No, it's fine. I just thought my life would be more than this.'

'We all have dreams, Reem, but we were children then. Come on, we used to say we would get married and live like they did in the movies we saw at the old cinema. Do you remember?'

'I don't remember that. Like you said, I was a kid.'

'Have you visited the British Museum?'

The subject switch threw Reem off, but Mahmoud didn't seem to notice.

'You should visit it. How about I meet you there? I will show you around. This Saturday?'

Reem couldn't help but agree. His eyes lit up in the way they did as a child. Before he left, she wanted to tell him how she did remember, how she remembered everything they shared. That she saw parts of him in the goodness of the people she met and how she was ashamed that she wasn't the woman she thought she'd become. But she didn't. She couldn't find the words.

Chapter 14

~ Leah ~

She hadn't seen Reem since the fire. Reem had told her that she and Inara had been rehoused in the shadow of the burnt-out block but Leah couldn't bring herself to return there. She wanted to meet Reem's baby and felt guilty that she hadn't, but she felt Reem wasn't ready. She couldn't stop crying when she'd told her about Elijah, so the two of them couldn't be strong together. Not yet, she thought. She didn't want to be reminded of the pain that carved its way through her body every time she thought of Elijah. The aching emptiness inside her body, inside her heart.

Everything reminded her of his face, his laugh, his life. Mostly, Leah wanted to sleep. When she closed her eyes, she closed the world around her. Inside her mind's eye, she could create a world where Elijah was still with her. When she imagined him, it was the most real thing she had to being next to him. She could hear his voice, she could see his smile, and could almost reach out and touch his skin. He laughed as he ran around the garden. He called her to him and she ran over, her hands outstretched to meet his. But when she was awoken, it felt as if she was dragged away from him. Her mum begged her not to spend all day and night in bed, but she ached to be next to him. When she was in the present world doing things that would 'make her feel better', the rooms filled with people and objects from wall to wall, everything felt empty. They were empty of his presence. He didn't run through the rooms. His voice didn't mix with the sounds of the day like it used to. His absence was everywhere.

After a few weeks had passed, the four walls of her bedroom seemed to enclose around her. Even the sweet dreams of Elijah were fading. To avoid being alone with her thoughts she left the house every day. She only knew how to do simple tasks that didn't require much thought. There was nothing else her body could do except to continue in what it had known before. It operated on autopilot, taking her through the manoeuvrings of her life before the fire.

Leah climbed the steps from the underground station and walked down the familiar streets of her old neighbourhood. Her footsteps echoed on the pavements, which was odd, she thought, since she felt like there was no weight behind her to make a sound. A van blared down the road. Leah stood back, automatically extending her right hand behind her to take his. To hold it, to keep him safe, out of danger. She left it hanging for a moment, before she realised he wasn't there. That was the problem with automatic functioning. Her body, her brain, every edge of every nerve still reached out to him as though he was still a part of her. Her reason for living. Her existence. Her footsteps made too much noise, they were too heavy to belong to her ghost of a body that had nothing left inside of it.

She slid the key into the lock and opened the door. Her existence as a cleaner at least meant she could work uninterrupted. No one was there to ask her about her loss. Somehow the scrubbing and polishing made her feel that she was working away at something. Cleansing. Removing the pain, if she could just do it for long enough. She could scrub the memory of that night away. Not his. Never his. She stopped. She closed her eyes and breathed deeply. She could still see him and smell him as though he was warm and close. It made her feel better. This is what she would hang onto; that he wasn't too far gone. There was nothing that the fire had left behind, except what Mo could tell her. She needed to ask him again. Did Elijah speak to him? Was he in pain? Did he know she wasn't there to protect him? The questions consumed her, so she worked faster.

Ray's dad's bed was empty. She dusted around, looking under the bed for his architect drawings – they had gone too. A funeral card with the date of his burial had been dropped on the floor. She imagined his burial. The coffin being lowered into the earth. His family throwing tokens in after him. Maybe they would throw in his old war medals. His wedding band. His drawings. Things they believed he wanted. The things they wanted to bury with him. The room had been painted. There were new blinds up by the window blocking the view. Through almost every window at the back of the house, Leah could see the tower. She wasn't sure if it was still smouldering in the daylight. She knew it couldn't be. The windows were empty holes, the new façade burnt away, revealing the skeleton of the building behind. Leah closed the blinds, but it reappeared in the other windows. She couldn't escape the shadow outside the window despite its distance; a stain on the landscape. A blot of grief against a pale sky. She calculated six floors up. She wondered if that was his bedroom window there, the one she was looking at. The garden courtyard jutted out, like a disused helipad. Nothing they had grown would have survived. She remembered the bees, and it was this thought that made her cry. She looked out of the window and imagined them soaring.

Maybe if she could speak to Mo, capture those last few seconds he had, that would help her. Leah heard the letterbox flap open and shut. An envelope landed on the doormat with her name written on it. Leah stepped over it and opened the front door.

'Emily? Is that you?' Leah called. She heard Emily's BMW speed off.

She picked up the letter from the floor and locked up behind her. She posted the spare key through the letterbox. She knew she wouldn't return to the house again.

~ Reem ~

Half dressed, half animal. Wings on backs. Horns protruding through heads. Feathers sprouting from their backs. Reem was dreaming. She must have been dreaming.

Chaos had descended onto the streets in a flurry of colours, skin and noise. The beat of drums thudded through her body, vibrating through her feet. Masqueraded dancers manoeuvred their way through the streets. Feathers, hidden faces, a horde of people packed together. The crowd moved and swarmed, becoming one mass of people, winding their way to the streets to the rhythm of the beating music hammering through her senses.

She was so sure she could feel it, that if she opened the door and reached out to touch someone, their body would be warm and soft and real. But she didn't dare open it because of what she might let inside. She hid under the blankets and tried to shut out the noise that came through the walls and the floors and the thin windows. The sound of glass shattering in the distance was followed by the sound of a trumpet being blown. No, a horn. Then, as if there was nothing there, silence descended. Absolute silence.

It began again, but she didn't want to look out of the window in case the sky was cracking, in case the moon had split into two and the stars were cascading down to the floor. She closed her eyes shut and imagined she was somewhere else. Somewhere far above, out of reach of the world that was falling down around her.

***

Reem arrived outside the British Museum later than they had arranged. Mahmoud was standing at the top of the steps, leaning up against a column. Groups of people milled past, guides in hand and taking photographs of the square with cameras. Mahmoud had put on his best suit. It looked like it was new. Reem stood debating, thinking of reasons why she couldn't go, but when he looked up and the flowers hung by his side, she noticed his gaze was still that of the familiar boy she knew from home.

'Are they yours?' Reem asked, pointing to the flowers scattered beneath them on the floor.

'No, no, I don't think so,' he laughed nervously. 'Shall we?'

Mahmoud led Reem inside and to her surprise, light streamed through the inside. Staircases twisted up to a blue-stained glass roof that flooded the central hall with light. She was completely engrossed, flitting from exhibit to exhibit. Every area beautifully curated and displayed. Perfectly dated in chronological order, the exhibitions snatched pieces of lost eras and centuries around the planet and made their stories come alive.

At the Ancient Egyptian exhibition, Reem marvelled at the remnants of the once strong, thriving cities. Depictions of their solidness, their huge extravagant palaces and riches. And underneath it all, they lay buried in pyramid tombs surrounded by their life's wealth. The way the mummies were wrapped in cloth, distorted, almost crumbled into dust, reminded her of the certainty of death. Death came to them despite their vast fortunes and royal bloodlines. Like an unspoken ghost, it crept into palaces, into chambers, into beds, and stole their lives. No power or riches could have stopped their souls from being pulled from their mouths. She wandered through, looking at their open mouths and their crooked neck bones, wondering if it was the force of their souls' exit that left them broken. All their scholars of mathematics, geometry, medicine and astronomy were laid to rest in open graves in a glass building, reminding people of an inevitable end. Reem knew the afterlife couldn't be bought with treasures, gold and precious jewels that belong to the Earth and its rightful Owner. Weaving through the exhibition, she was reminded of the Qur'anic stories she was told as a child. The story of Moses, who was sent down the River Nile in a basket, only to become the ruler of Egypt. She thought of Adar. She would be reunited with him. Reem remembered a *hadith* of the Prophet Muhammad: '*You will be with those you love.*'

It was as though the reminders of the ancient past, the promises of what would come to those who are patient, came alive in those rooms.

In the Middle Eastern exhibition, a tour of the oldest pages of the Qur'an were on display. They had been discovered in the text of an old Egyptian document and were uncovered by a PhD researcher based only a couple of hundred miles away in the city of Birmingham. The pages lay open inside a glass cabinet, roped off, but she was close enough to read the familiar verse that was written on the old pages of animal parchment paper. Reem never tired of hearing how the researcher had found them between pages of an old Egyptian text, only to discover that they didn't belong there. The parchment had been carbon dated back to the time of the Prophet's companions. Yet more proof to her that the Qur'an's message stood the test of time.

It was as if all the history, all the glass displays capturing bygone eras, the exhumed treasures and the fallen cities – none of it was as powerful to her as the revelation that stood through time. When cities had gone, rich kings had died, powerful rulers had disappeared and left only remnants of their greatness, she came to terms with the fact that she no longer held the crumbling ruins of her city in her apartment. What she could take from the country was not in the land itself – it existed in her religion, her culture and within her.

Mahmoud stood back and allowed her to take in the history. She knew he had chosen to visit this place entirely for her. He intrinsically knew, even after all these years, what she needed. He smiled at her knowingly. They may have looked different, but underneath they were the same. They belonged to the same place and the same shared history united them.

The next exhibition was on Middle Eastern antiques. Reem peered into the glass, running her fingers over the top as if she could feel the rough stone, the clay pots underneath, the blue jewels that reminded her of her mother. But the dates didn't match.

'This isn't right.'

'What is it?' Mahmoud said, pushing a sleeping Inara over in her stroller.

'This isn't the right dates for this piece. Look at it. Remember when we found this near the heritage site, the old palace?'

Mahmoud shrugged his shoulders. 'I think I remember something about that.'

'And this one here,' Reem said, already moving on to the next artefact. 'It isn't for cooking! Can you imagine our mothers using this?'

Mahmoud laughed. 'You know I was never one for being in the kitchen. Just the woodshed.'

'Yes, and you wouldn't have used this,' Reem said, pointing to a sharp object.

'That doesn't look like anything I would have used in this century.'

Reem had attracted the notice of a curator who was taking a tour behind her.

'Excuse me, David here. I helped curate this exhibition.'

'Oh, hello. Sorry, I didn't mean for you to hear.'

'No, no, that isn't what I meant,' he said, pushing his thick spectacles back and pulling out a pen from the ink-stained pockets of his brown tweed coat. 'I did wonder about this one. You know, it's difficult out of context. We don't always get it right. What are your thoughts on this?'

Reem explained what she thought, what century it belonged to. It was not too out of date, but it was, according to her knowledge, in the wrong exhibit.

'What are your credentials in this field?'

'I was studying Middle Eastern history, before I had to leave.'

David pushed his glasses up his nose and scrawled onto his notepad.

'Excuse me, sir? Can we continue?'

One of the group members, wearing a museum tag around his neck, had approached and seemed eager to get the tour back on track as the students had started to wander off.

'Yes, of course. Erm – your name, I didn't catch it.'

'Reem Ahmad.'

'Reem, could you come and visit me when my schedule clears up? I have some more artefacts in the back I could do with some help on. Here is my card. We have much more behind the scenes.'

Reem nodded, a mixture of emotions flooding through her. There was something about the stale preservation of history that made her feel uneasy. There was something about the glass cabinetry, the way it held things prisoner. Like a heart kept in a jar, it wasn't where it was supposed to go. But she agreed nonetheless. How could she not, she thought.

Chapter 15

~ Leah ~

L eah sat on the end of her bed, dressed in the outfit her mum had laid out earlier. She had no energy to resist anything. Instead she went from place to place, in an almost non-existent way, hoping she would eventually fade into the curtains or sink into the floor. There was no pleasure in her life anymore. Sometimes she thought she heard Elijah shout her, so she would run downstairs and fling open the garden doors and hunt for him as he played hide and seek in the trees. She hadn't seen him since she put him to bed that night and despite what the doctors told her, it was entirely plausible to her that he would walk in at any moment. She would tell him off for making her sick with worry, but they would hug and her arms would reach around his perfect, warm body and she would kiss his honey-coloured cheek and never let him go.

Leah walked out to the bottom of the garden and opened the door to the cabin filled with Elijah's toys. The cabin smelt of damp wood, the smell that she would try and wash out of his clothes when he spent the afternoon in there. The unused bikes and toys stood motionless like skeletons, refracting the dull light barely breaking through the window. Leah spun the wheel of the bike around, listening to it clicking. She remembered that he had wanted to sleep over. If only she had let him sleep over there with her parents. If she wasn't so stubborn. Maybe it would have been different. Maybe he would have been there with her in the cabin and together they'd grieve for those they'd lost. At least then, his hand would have been in hers and she would be able to feel the heart beating in his chest and the blood pumping through his veins. But there was nothing left. Only the faint hope that Reem had consoled her with, that he was above the skies. How the stars were the lamps to the first heaven. It made her feel that Elijah was close to her. That he could see the same brightness in the blinding darkness.

'Leah, Reem is here,' she heard her mother call from in the house. 'Ah, isn't she a darling! Here, let Mary take her,' Barbara said, lifting Inara from Reem's arms. 'Leah is outside. She's been sat there all day.'

Leah wiped away her tears and opened the cabin door. Reem was already on her way to her, walking determinedly.

'Leah,' Reem said, throwing her arms around Leah's unresponsive body. 'Can I sit with you?' Reem ducked through the door, disturbing the dust by trying to find somewhere to sit.

'They are launching an official investigation into the accident,' Reem said, pausing for a response. 'Mo, Ali and Nidal were the first ones there. They were leaving *taraweeh* prayers at midnight so they were awake *Subhan'Allah*. Ali is still in hospital. So is Nidal. Third degree burns to their bodies.' Reem cleared her throat.

'How are you? Are you hurt?'

'I wasn't there,' said Reem quietly.

The change in her voice made Leah take notice. 'How come?'

'Because of my husband, Leah. His name was Nazim. He wasn't a nice man, really –'

'Wait, hold on. You're married?' Leah stood up from the chair, leaning on it for support. 'What do you mean you're married? You never told me?'

'I just didn't know how to bring it up and I thought I had seen the last of him when I left home.'

'So wait,' Leah said, dragging her chair until it was closer to Reem's, 'was he in England? Did you expect him?'

'No, he's from my hometown in Syria. There's no way I expected him. But that night, after the Big Iftar, I went home and he had let himself in. He was his usual threatening self, and of course, I was worried about the baby, I was in pain – I didn't want to go to the hospital... they remind me of... something that I haven't quite got the full picture of.'

'So where did you go? I would have helped.'

'I know, a doctor, right? My first choice...'

'Except I can't seem to help anyone I love.'

'Leah, you are only a doctor.'

'What do you mean?'

'It isn't up to you who lives and dies. You can only do your best, that's all.'

Leah nodded. She hadn't thought of it like that before. 'I guess, but with Matthew there were signs.'

'Yes, and even if you did notice them, what could you have done?'

Leah shrugged her shoulders. 'I don't trust myself anymore.' Feeling like she had revealed too much, Leah changed the direction of the conversation. 'So, where did you go?'

'I went to work. And guess where she was born?'

'No! Not at the hotel?'

'Yes, born into the life of a maid,' Reem laughed.

Leah smiled. 'So where is your husband now?'

'They found a body matching his description in my apartment. He died in the fire.'

'But you aren't sure?'

Reem shrugged her shoulders. 'I can't even seem to trust my own mind these days. But I know logically it makes sense – he was there, he hasn't been seen, I haven't heard from him – but I don't feel free yet. It feels like there is something else. Something else I need to discover and I don't know where that feeling is coming from.'

'Time will tell,' Leah said.

'What about tonight? Your mum mentioned Jonathan is taking you out. That isn't like you.'

Leah pulled her mouth upside down.

'So why go?'

'I don't have the energy to fight with her anymore. And he told me he had something to tell me. Some good news apparently, and I could do with that, whatever it is.'

'So you've quit your cleaning job?'

'I didn't need to. Emily left me a heartfelt note.' Leah passed the envelope to Reem, who read it aloud.

'"Your services are no longer required." Oh.'

'Yep, that's my friends for me.'

'Not me,' Reem said, 'you can come and clean for me anytime.'

Leah broke a smile.

'We'd better go in before they come looking for us,' Reem said, and together they went and sat next to each other in the middle of the dining table. The doorbell played a tune, breaking their solace. Leah could hear her mum ushering guests inside.

'She said she wasn't inviting anyone else. This is so typical of her.'

'Oh, I hope you don't mind,' Barbara burst in, 'but a few guests are joining us. You remember Charles, the doctor, and his wife, Stella. Reem?'

Reem didn't respond, but Leah could tell by the look on her face that she remembered exactly who he was.

~ Reem ~

When Charles came in, he walked straight over to Reem and kissed both her cheeks. She was too startled to pull away. He smelt of alcohol and another stronger smell that Reem couldn't decipher despite it being familiar. Sickening.

'Excuse me,' Reem said, pushing out her chair and escaping to the room adjacent. She began looking for exits and now, after the fire, she noticed how stark the differences were. The doors were fire doors. The solid, wooden window frames provided escape routes down onto the streets. The heavy bricks used to build the house seemed inflammable. There was an expanse of grass outside the window. Miles of ground to escape to. No crowds of people, scattering like moths, trying to find the way out. No children sleeping multiple storeys high into the night sky with only one way out. No tight hallways and spirals of stairs filled with choking smoke. Her mouth was open, trying to inhale deeper breaths, but the air didn't seem to be reaching her lungs.

Charles appeared behind her and closed the door shut. She tried to leave the room, but he stood in the doorway.

'You look familiar to me, young girl.'

'Get away from me,' Reem said, trying to squeeze under the arm that he had pinned to the wall. The smell from his skin was now nauseating.

'Would I have seen you before?'

'Yes, at the last one of these,' Reem said, instantly regretting coming.

His breath was heavy with the smell of alcohol. But his skin, it smelt of something stronger. Reem closed her eyes and breathed deeply as a memory returned to her. A place where she had been before. A place where she had inhaled that same smell in the air. She was back in the sea, the waves thick and heavy. The air filled with screams. She stood back, uneasy on her feet. He came closer.

'No, that isn't it. I can't quite place you.' His eyes gaped as he remembered. 'I knew it since the last time I saw you. I've been racking my brains, but of course, I see hundreds.' He stopped, backed off and stumbled as though the memory came with force. 'You were supposed to be coming with the young lad but he never showed. Cost me thousands.'

'What are you talking about?' Reem tried to move away from him but her legs almost buckled beneath her. Her body began to shake uncontrollably.

'Now where is that snake, Nazim? He still owes me money. Well, you can make up for your little brother now.'

Reem heard the door open and thought she could hear Leah's voice, but she couldn't be sure. Her heart was racing, and her mind was trying to fix everything into place.

'Charles, what are you doing?'

'Oh nothing, just catching up with your help,' Charles replied, falling backwards.

Reem felt herself being pulled away as Charles poured another drink. She heard the clang of a ring against the glass and turned to look. The ring on his finger. She remembered where she had seen it before. She broke free out of Leah's arms, ran out the back doors and threw up in the flowers.

'Oh goodness, Reem, what on earth is the matter?' Leah said, snapping into her training mode. She pulled back her hair, felt her forehead and encouraged her to kneel.

'It's him,' she said. 'I know where I recognise him from. He was on the boat. The boat they damaged.'

Reem looked towards the house and saw Charles staggering up the stairs.

'Oh God, no. Inara.' Reem bolted inside and snatched Inara. She ran straight out of the front door, staring back at the mansion lit up from inside against the blackness. Inside, the people looked like ghosts, moving about between the windows.

Haunted by the smell and the realisation that something terrible had happened, she began to run. She didn't stop until she reached home. But home didn't feel safe enough. She needed a person, someone who could protect them. If she could work it out then Charles could, and she couldn't help but calculate what they both may be worth. Now Nazim wasn't here to give the orders and with lives like theirs being up for sale, she felt like she wasn't safe.

She banged on the doors on the tower block next to hers. She couldn't remember which one Mo and Nidal lived at. Doors opened, lights flickered on. Strangers' faces shouted at her through the cracks, until finally, Nidal came out.

'Reem, is that you?'

'*Alhamdulilah*, you're here. Please let us in.'

Reem barged past him with Inara now crying under arm. 'Help us. He's coming for us.'

'What's going on, bro? Check them over, see if they're hurt,' Mo said.

Reem lay on the floor with Inara next to her, and certain she was now away from Charles, away from everything that she had seen, she fell asleep from pure exhaustion.

~ Leah ~

The doorbell rang just as Reem ran out into the garden. She kept thinking she needed to follow her, but she was stuck. Jonathan was stood in the doorway, insistent as usual. Reem was already out of view. She had never seen Reem drink before, but maybe she had? Or maybe she was embarrassed about how she had found her and Charles in the study? She told herself she would find out in the morning, but she still felt deeply unsettled.

Jonathan had booked a table at her favourite restaurant. She hadn't been there since she met Matthew. The room was dimly lit, decorated with rich hues of purple and dark Malaysian wood. The tables were a decent distance apart, allowing privacy between the couples. Bare light bulbs hung low from timber frames and each table was laid with a white table cloth, pressed into triangles at the corners. Tucked underneath them were leather armchairs. The room had the quiet hush of a discreet meeting place. She wasn't sure she should be there. It felt like betrayal. She thought of Reem.

'I remembered you liked this place,' Jonathan said, after ordering on her behalf. 'Do you remember when we used to come here after our university lectures?'

'Yes, that seems like a lifetime ago.'

'It does, doesn't it? But there is always time. You should go back and finish your training. You have less than a year left,' Jonathan said as he folded his napkin into small pieces, 'in fact, I hope you don't mind, but my father spoke to the hospital and told them about your situation.' He stopped.

'What exactly is my situation?' Leah snapped.

'Just that you are on compassionate leave, that's all. Leah, I am on your side.'

Leah relaxed a little and sipped some water.

'I'm sorry. You said you had good news?'

'Yes, the board at the hospital have agreed for you to complete your training with them at the hospital. All you have to do is call this man here. They arranged it after my father spoke to them on your behalf. A little persuading by me didn't go amiss,' Jonathan said, sipping champagne and looking pleased with himself. 'Here's his business card. Just call him when you're ready.'

Leah's stomach flipped. The hospital where Elijah was last. The hospital where she had said goodbye. She slipped the business card into her handbag. 'You've been at the house a lot recently,' Leah said, changing the subject.

'Yes, I'm helping Phil out after that disastrous event at the council. He will probably lose it all.'

'What do you mean?' Leah realised that Jonathan had no idea that she had lived there. Her parents would never say. They said Elijah had had 'an accident' and he hadn't pressed further. Living there was obviously too much of an embarrassment for her mum and dad to admit to. Typical, she thought, wondering why she still felt disappointed.

'Yes, yes. What area was that again?' Leah pried, hoping it wasn't obvious that her dad hadn't told her anything about it. The food was delivered to the table by two waiters setting up trays by their sides and opening up silver cloches, before serving them at the table. Leah knew he had ordered the most expensive starters on the menu. She had eaten them regularly once, but she hadn't eaten them in years. It smelt too rich, too creamy. It turned her stomach. She had barely eaten in the last few weeks and her bland cooking was something she had gotten used to.

'You were saying about the council?'

'Oh yes,' Jonathan said between mouthfuls. He stopped and self-consciously dabbed his chin, regaining his composure. 'Well, you know my father runs the investment house.'

'The one you are a partner in, yes.'

'Yes, exactly,' he said, leaning back in his chair and arching his back, pausing so Leah could focus on that. 'After the mistake, well, your dad voted for it to be used, didn't he?'

'Yes, I remember him saying.'

'So now with all the lawsuits that may be coming his way, after the cladding ordeal –'

'The cladding?'

'Yes, they wanted to save money, of course, so Phil arranged for this contractor to do the work. Saved them thousands. But after the fire, well. You can only imagine.'

'Not just imagine. All those people lost their lives.'

'It isn't so much that, no. It's more the problem if they sue. Excuse me. Waiter!' Jonathan clicked his fingers. 'We need more champagne, please.'

'Don't bother ordering for me,' Leah said as she went to stand up, but she felt Jonathan pull her hand down. 'How can you say that?'

'I didn't mean it badly. I mean, it's really sad and everything but do you realise that it's going to screw your dad over? I thought you'd care.'

'Not when it ended like this. He deserves it.'

'You don't have to act so defensive and push people away all the time –'

'You don't know me.'

'You don't know yourself. You spend so much time avoiding everything that could be good for you, as though you want to be a victim your whole life.' Jonathan's voice was now a strained whisper, the tension making the vein in his neck pop out as he tried to maintain his decorum.

'What do you mean?'

'Oh come on, Leah. A cleaner! What a joke, when you're almost qualified to be a doctor.'

Leah blushed. She had no idea Jonathan knew about her job. 'It's only temporary. I was – I needed to...' Leah stopped to take a sip of water.

'I know that instead of concentrating on moving on after your last mistake, you're determined to throw away your future.'

'Don't you dare mention him as a mistake.'

'I didn't necessarily mean Matthew,' he said, grabbing her arm as she pushed out her chair to stand up.

'I'd rather have nothing than be as inhuman as people like you, my parents, Emily. I don't want anything to do with any of you. I'm not going to sell my soul for the cheap price you put on it.'

Leah threw down her napkin and yanked her arm free. She threw down money that clattered on the table. The coins fell into her dinner, but she didn't care. All she wanted to do was leave him and the world she had known, the world she was once a part of, behind her.

Leah couldn't go back to her parents. She couldn't face them. She didn't know how true it was and she was in denial that her dad could be involved. She thought back to the hushed conversations with her mum, the insistence that she move out of there. The fact that they had called the social worker to have Elijah removed. Did they know back then that it was dangerous? She walked through the empty streets as the rain began to fall, soaking her clothes and forcing her to feel something. The cold set in. She wouldn't return there. She had nothing left to say to them. She could never be part of that life anymore. As she walked, she passed her old house. She stood outside it. It was empty. There were no lights on. On closer inspection, she saw the paint was flaking on the outside and the weeds were forcing their way up through the grass. She finally understood what she would have to give up to have the house again, and it wasn't the life she wanted. It was worth nothing now she was alone.

The rain created a mist off the pavement and the moon shone brightly behind it, casting a large shadow on the street. Leah walked away, into the light of the street lamps. Under their soft, warm glow, she saw a glimpse of another future waiting for her.

Chapter 16

~ *Reem* ~

In the morning, the light filtered through the charred tower, creating a silhouette in the room. Reem awoke with a start. She grabbed at Inara under the blankets and looked around. After a few minutes, satisfied with the safety of where she was, she relaxed. But the sick feeling clung to her insides.

Mo and Nidal listened to her speak. They didn't interrupt once. Mo maintained a concerned frown, seemingly unnerved, whereas the anger in Nidal's eyes grew with every sentence.

'I'm going to the police,' Nidal said.

'Please don't. If he finds out I know for sure, I don't know what he will do.' She paused. 'Adar, he was there, I remember. I thought I saw him leave on a lorry, but I must have been wrong, I must have blocked it out. Something else came back to me. The waves. He... is it possible to have imagined that he was still with me? That he was still alive?' Reem sobbed.

'Anything is possible after that type of trauma,' Mo said softly.

'I didn't think it would be him back on the Tube that day,' Nidal said.

'Why would you think that?'

'Come on bro, ain't nobody gonna be bumping into someone on the Tube that's been missing for months.'

Reem cried. She felt like she had been living in a daze. She couldn't trust her own mind anymore. The images it created. She wanted it so badly to be him, that she had forced it.

'I need to do something,' Nidal said, standing up and beginning to pace the room.

'Let's work this out. If what Reem says is true, then this is dangerous stuff.'

'I'm sick of being scared about what people say, man. Enough of this. It's wrong and I never say nothing. Nah bruv, that's it. I'm outing it.' Nidal stormed out.

'Nidal, wait, come on! Don't act in anger, you'll only regret it.'

'I ain't living in fear no more, bro. Allah got my back. I'm gonna start doing what I should have done a long time ago. Chantelle was right about me and now she ain't even here for me to apologise to.'

Reem sensed that Mo wanted to go after him but he couldn't leave her in this state. So Reem got up and dusted herself down.

'Nidal's right. Allah will protect us, Mo. Take us home.'

Across the grass, Reem saw Leah hanging around outside the front door. She looked like she hadn't slept all night.

'Oh goodness, Reem, are you okay? I was so worried.' She turned to look at Mo, 'Mo, hi. I haven't seen you in a while. Since...' Leah paused and patted down her hair, trying to unknot it at the back where it had been soaked in the rain. She gave up when she reached her damp clothes, realising she was beyond a quick fix.

'Since the fire. I'm sorry, Leah. I am sorry. I tried but I was too late.' Mo didn't look at her. He kept shielding his eyes with the palm of his hand. 'Look, I have to go, yeah.'

Before Leah could answer, Mo had turned around and was pacing through the grass with his head down.

'Mo, wait! Please!' Leah shouted after him.

'Come on, Leah, let's go inside. You need to change. You must be freezing out here,' Reem said, sensing she probably shouldn't say any more at that moment.

Reem watched Leah's eyes switch from Mo to the burnt out tower.

'I haven't seen it this close since... God. Look at it.' Leah couldn't turn her eyes away. 'Dear God, I can't believe anyone survived.' She couldn't stop the tears streaming down her face. 'My baby... my baby...'

Reem managed to get her and Inara inside. Reem hurried and found dry clothes for Leah. She had never seen her look so ill.

'I'm sorry I left you, Reem. I should've come with you. Please forgive me.'

'You weren't to know. I didn't even know until...'

'What happened last night with Charles? Did he hurt you?'

Reem stayed silent. She didn't know what to say.

'Oh God, what is he involved in?' Leah said, her hands clasped over her mouth.

'I remembered what happened on the boat. Why the smell made me feel sick, where I had seen the ring on his left hand. All of it came back to me.'

Reem screamed out loud. Leah held her silently. Neither of them had any words left.

chapter 17

~ *Reem* ~

As Reem uncovered her secrets, vivid nightmares returned. Sometimes she shot up in the night, feeling scars behind her kidneys that weren't there. Or she imagined Inara stolen in the night. As she began to force herself to recall what had passed, she allowed memories of her past to filter in. She saw the ruins of what she had left behind in Syria. The reasons why she'd left.

The coin she had kept in her pocket all this time had given her the first clue to unravelling what had really happened on her journey. She flattened the newspaper sheet it was wrapped in to read the story printed on the page. It told of refugees being driven away in lorries, hidden in the back as they were smuggled through borders. But it wasn't Adar's face she saw peering out of the back of the lorry; it was the news report of another boy's fate. 'Funnel Logistics' was painted on the side. Subconsciously, her mind was adopting refugee stories that were becoming part of her own memories and experiences. The stories of what was happening to Syrian refugees played out and morphed into what she believed were her own memories, filling in the gaps that were too traumatic for her to remember. There were huge gaps in her memory and it was becoming impossible to know the truth behind them.

Reem worked closely with Nidal. He began his work the moment Reem told him the beginning of what she remembered, on that evening when she ran to theirs. Her memory triggered from the remembrance of Charles had now begun to open up the truth. A truth Nidal also wanted to tell the world because, as he explained to Reem, he had a duty to share the atrocities of what they wanted hidden. Every time Reem saw fear creep in, she told Nidal to quit but he told her he was determined to bring it to the surface, no matter the cost.

Gradually, as the weeks passed, Reem's memory began to restore. She was assigned a counsellor specialising in Post Traumatic Stress Disorder. A survival technique of the brain meant she was diagnosed with a symptom of PTSD that resulted in temporary amnesia, an avoidance of anyone or anything that may relate to the past. It also explained her obsession with collectables – it was a way of keeping home close to her. In the safety of her counsellor's room, she began to explore the recesses of her brain that had been shut down to protect her.

Over the weeks, Nidal began to reveal her story and the journey of others. He researched further, he interviewed refugees and migrants, he travelled to the port town where Reem had been found, he spoke with search and rescue boats and visited pawn shops and places that sold Syrian antiquities to see if they could shed light on the story. Nidal pieced the rest of the story together from other accounts. Human traffickers told him how they took large payments, usually in the form of cash, gold, antiques and other valuables. Families sold everything they had, everything they had collected over lifetimes in order to get themselves or their loved ones out of the country. Some stories surfaced that land and homes were sold, with deeds being handed over to those profiting from war. Nidal published the truth, three months after Reem had arrived at his place and told him her story. The truth was worse than any of them imagined. The article told of a scheme that was so well-orchestrated, so profitable and so dark, that it would change them all. It set off a chain of events that would determine the rest of their lives.

The refugees' journeys were thought to be well-known. The outcome of their plight was widely reported and the country was still reeling from the images of the drowned boy who had washed up on the beach. Of the traumatised child sitting in the back of an ambulance, barely able to speak. The news flashed images of scores of refugees, pushed back from coastlines, left to drown when land was barely a few miles away as countries shut down their coasts. But what Reem was beginning to reveal had only been spoken about in whispers.

The journeys started in the familiar pattern of rubber dinghy boats leaving the mainland. They were told that they would sail out to meet a bigger ship that would cross the sea to reach European shores. But what no one knew was that when the dinghies were out of sight from the coast, the passengers spotted divers underneath them. No one could understand why there would be divers under the dinghy. Reem remembered seeing the diving gear, just under the waves. She stared at them, her mind trying to work out why they were there. Then the flash of spears in their hand. It wasn't until Reem saw them stabbing them through the boat that she realised what was happening. The boat began to fill with water, screams of panic erupted around them, but they were too far off the coast to be heard and too far out to sea to be noticed. There was a ship waiting for them in the distance. It was so close. Maybe it was a way of getting everyone off the dinghy. After all, there were no boards or planks to walk up, just a ladder on the side and most of the passengers were wearing lifejackets.

Children clung desperately to their parents. She couldn't see Adar. An elderly couple were the first to fall over the sides as the boat took on water. Their arms outstretched, their hands clasped together. They had no energy left to fight, and Reem watched them as they drifted further away, disappearing behind the waves. She glanced back at the ship. It sat silently in the water, unmoving. They could make it to the ship, she thought. But as they hit the water, one by one, the waves seemed to grow and swell. People were drowning in front of her. The crew on the ship were shouting to one another in panic. A lifeboat crashed into the water. It dropped on its side, flipped over, and landed in the waves with a crash upside down. They were panicking too much, they were losing people. Reem would only later discover why that mattered to them.

They managed to deploy another boat and dragged the limp, almost drowned survivors onto the boat. Reem saw the children being picked up first. They dragged the youngsters in first and went up in age, leaving the eldest until last. Reem was pulled out onto the deck of the ship. She looked at it. It had a cross painted in red on the main deck, on the walls. It looked like it used to be a hospital ship of some sort. When the panic had subsided and everyone was out of the water, the crew did a headcount. They shouted at each other. Some were missing. They pulled Reem up. She was supposed to be with someone. They noticed the roundness in her stomach. She was sent to one side. Relief set in and the survivors started thanking the crew, reassured that they were on the last leg of the journey. Soon they would see European shores; they were saved and together they began to allow themselves to dream of a new future.

But Reem felt uneasy. She had been watching the crew, who seemed increasingly anxious. The way they communicated with one another, the way they kept their faces hidden, the stiff walk they employed that she had only ever seen before on military-trained men. The ship didn't move. Hours passed. Most of the survivors had fallen asleep. Slumped on one another. Night came. Eventually, the doors to the lower deck opened and they were told to go underneath. Reem waited until last. There was something about disappearing from under the sky, the wide expanse of space. The soothing lull of the moonlight. Under the deck she could see it was dark. It smelt damp, medicinal. The passengers squeezed through the doorway, the sheer number of them barely able to get through the door. Exhausted, thirsty, hungry. But no one imagined it could get worse. Yet what waited for them was an evil that no one with any hope left could have imagined.

Underneath the deck, makeshift bunks had been placed next to each other. Rows and rows of beds. Next to each bed was a stainless steel trolley. On the trolley was a kidney dish and scalpels. It took a few moments for the scene to sink in, before mayhem broke loose. The ones at the front surged forward, attacking the crew; the women and children looked behind for somewhere to escape but the doors were shut. The sound of metal operating equipment clattered as it fell onto the floor. The crew seemed to double in size, faceless doctors wearing scrubs entered with needles. Reem saw the passengers drop one by one. All their rage and fear crumpled to the floor as their legs gave way beneath them and their bodies lay alive, but motionless. They were lifted onto the beds.

Reem crouched down in the corner as the stench of sick and urine overtook her senses. She closed her eyes shut to escape the scene. She felt a sharp pinch in her am. She yanked it away, opening her eyes to a gloved hand, an empty syringe dropped on the floor. The scene moved in clouds. She was drugged but not enough that it knocked her unconscious. She couldn't move her body but she could see, hear, smell. She saw the tin buckets of fresh ice, heard the sound of running water, smelt the metallic air heavy with blood. She could see the passengers being operated on, their organs removed and packed up and their bodies tipped over the side. One after another, the surgeon expertly removed organs as though the people in front of them were just bodies, already dead. Except Reem knew they weren't. Eyes moved. Hands that hung down the sides of the beds twitched helplessly. Tears dropped. One after another, a conveyor belt of souls. Torn apart. Parts of them packaged up. The parts of them they could sell. The parts of them they couldn't were sealed in glass jars of chemicals. The remains were thrown into the sea, sinking deep below its depths into the abyss.

Reem lay motionless. Helpless. Watching and waiting for it to be her turn as the surgeon moved closer and closer. Through the haziness, her eyes caught sight of a gold ring on the surgeon's left hand as he waved it in front of her eyes to see if she was conscious. His piercing eyes peered over the surgeon's mask, until she saw one bright shining light, then blackness surrounded her. She imagined that she was back under the night sky, and the light was the moon.

Reem woke up in a hospital bed. She had been found by the coast of a major port town. She was barely alive; no documents, no survivors, no history of how she had arrived. No Adar. Just a few miles down the shore they found her belongings. Shortly after her arrival, a damaged boat had been found with no reported survivors. They'd assumed that was where she had come from.

The counsellor said it would take time for the gaps to fill in, and often she would be triggered by a smell or a sound. That's how her memories returned. She remembered Charles.

She couldn't avoid him after that. His face was on every news channel and on every newspaper in the stands. Wherever she turned, it seemed like his face was there. Only this time, he was exposed. He couldn't hide anymore and everyone knew what he was capable of. Charles was arrested but the court case was dismissed, citing no official evidence. However, after that he was unable to practise medicine, lost his licence and left the country. Nidal's story reported that surgeons were being recruited from all continents and were paid tens of thousands of pounds to be part of the trade. Once they reported the dinghy as being sunk off the coast, they would be forgotten about. The countries didn't help drowning refugees, so those who had been assumed dead at sea were forgotten about completely. Their numbers unknown. Nidal and Reem had no idea how many had been affected. How could they? Their plan was that the bodies were lost at sea and so never recovered. The official lists of those missing from Syria alone topped over sixty thousand. Since there were barely any survivors it had gone unnoticed for months, even years. Reem thought about the number of missing persons. Adar was one of them. She never did recollect seeing him there in the beds, of being operated on. He could have been – her view was limited and her memories shattered into disconnected pieces. She realised afterwards, after what Charles had said, that Nazim had paid for her safe passage. If it wasn't for Inara, she may never have survived. It was in this moment that Reem realised her life was out of her control. She felt the impermanence of the safety and stability that had once accompanied her childhood and had quickly dissipated as she grew. She had no idea that war could bring so much horror. She took some temporary solace in the fact that with the revelation out, that was the end.

***

Nidal's article went viral. Death threats alternated with messages of support on his social media. Many came forward to inquire about their missing family members. It became too big for Nidal. He cancelled his social media accounts and went off the grid. He handed over the information he had to the police. He told Reem he had been offered large sums of cash to withdraw the story, to claim it was fabricated. But he told Reem that money couldn't buy his soul. It belonged to only One. Reem took comfort in that. She often went back to the night when he told her that, when it became hard for her to cope. Yet at the time she didn't know she would have to, because she had no idea of what was to come.

It was an ordinary weekday night. Reem was at home with Inara and Leah. Reem had cooked dinner and they were sitting in the lounge, flicking through the TV channels, avoiding the news, trying to find something that would take their mind off the increasingly longer nights. Reem didn't know why, but she decided to go to *Isha* prayers at the mosque. She needed a break in her routine. Inara was usually awake or Leah was out and she couldn't take her, but tonight it all fitted into place. She did *wudu*, then put on her coat and scarf over her floor-length *abaya*. She rushed out, noticing that the prayers would start soon, and in her haste, she hadn't kissed Inara goodbye.

The call to prayer rang out inside the mosque. She had made it in time and stood with a handful of other sisters in the prayer room. Laila had come. The *imam* led the prayers and his voice crackled through the speakers from the men's section. Reem took solace in the unrushed prayers when she was led by an *imam* in the mosque. She found peace in the longer recitations of the Qur'an after each *surah*, and the pure concentration she had from being out of the flat, or of potentially being walked in on back at the hotel.

When the prayer had finished she sat with Laila, who consoled Reem with the only words she knew. 'Allah will find a way. Don't give up hope, *habibte.*'

And just as the words of hope left Laila's lips, there was an almighty smash outside of the mosque, followed by gunshots. 'Get down!' Laila shouted, covering Reem's head with her arms. They lay on the mosque floor as silence fell outside, only for a brief second, and then the screams started.

They ran to the door and opened it to a scene Reem's eyes could barely believe. Laila screamed and ran out to the bodies on the floor. Reem stayed where she was, watching in horror as people moaned on the floor in pain. They needed help. They needed a doctor. It took Reem a few seconds to know what to do. She called Leah. She crouched down, the phone shaking in her hand and every now and then Reem tried to leap forward to help, but her own body froze entirely on the spot. Her eyes couldn't recognise the broken figures that lay on the street in front of the mosque. She hadn't even noticed Leah arriving and shoving Inara into her arms. Reem was stirred into action upon seeing her and put her in the safety of the mosque before stumbling back outside, finally able to see what was happening.

Nidal was crushed under a van. His body was half sticking out from under its tyre. Another man was slumped behind the wheel. A gunshot to his head. But Reem had heard multiple gunshots. She looked around. Mo had been shot. Ali too.

'Nidal, hold on. An ambulance is on its way,' Leah said, taking off her jacket and trying to keep him warm.

Leah then ran over to Mo. He was losing consciousness. She shouted for Reem to take off her scarf. Leah wrapped it around his shoulder, stemming the blood. She dragged him over to the steps by the mosque to elevate his body. Then she ran to Ali and put him in the recovery position, her hand pressing down on the gunshot wound in his leg. The pavement was littered with debris. The pure white cloth of their prayer clothes now stained deep red. Reem ran over to Nidal and held him in his arms. The same way she had held Adar that night. Nidal held his right forefinger to the sky and shortly after, he smiled. A smile that lingered as his soul was eased from his body.

Reem wondered why she couldn't feel the cold anymore. Suddenly it became a warm night, humid, like the nights back home. Crippled by the sight of blood and shrapnel, Reem's eyes closed tightly shut. Trying to block out the horror unfolding in front of her. It came to her, not like her imagined memories had, but as lucid as a flash of lightning, battering through her consciousness.

It was a scene similar to this one. It was night time. The lights in the street cast pools of white onto the street, and under the serene sounds of crickets and the gentle flicker of the fire warming the courtyard, Reem heard it. It sliced through the sky with so much force that it sounded as though it was being torn open. Deep thuds followed before blinding shots of fire leapt into the air, one after another, sending the walls crashing to the ground. The houses collapsed under the sheer force. The street outside the courtyard gates was ablaze. Frightened screams curdled the thin night time air and Reem crouched down. Her body froze to the floor as debris rained down. Her mum's hands and face jutted out from underneath a pile of stones that had crumbled from the house. Her dad's coffee cup was smashed to pieces on the floor.

'Adar,' her mum called. It was the last thing she ever said. Reem turned to look at the pomegranate tree. Hanging from it, a misshapen fruit. Blood red, with threads hanging down dangled from the branches. She moved closer. It wasn't fruit. It was a shoe. Its laces hanging down in the branches. Stained red. Reem looked closer and held it in her hand. It was Adar's shoe. Filled with blood.

Reem realised now that the reason she kept thinking of Adar walking to the mosque barefoot is because she had found his shoe, bloodied in the pomegranate tree. On a night like this one. One that had started so easily, so normally. And now more people she loved were injured, dying outside of the mosque. That was where she had found the rest of Adar. He had died from an airstrike back home, the night before they were supposed to leave together. The bombs hit the house, demolished the streets, and out of her whole family, she was the only one who had escaped. Adar had died on the cold floor, on the doorstep of the mosque.

The ambulance arrived, its sirens piercing the night time air. Mo and Ali survived. But she knew Nidal had already left this world behind. In pieces.

Chapter 18

~ *Reem* ~

It turned into a cruel, cold winter. The nights grew shorter. The fog rolled in, and the heaving clouds and dark nights reflected the grief of the community. The landscape shifted around them. Reem couldn't turn on the TV without seeing the news of how the world was shifting. Trump had been elected President over in the USA and throughout Europe, bans on Muslim dress were being turned into law. Reem flicked through the channels until they became a montage of protesters. Images of women with their hair and faces covered with bold, red crosses struck across their faces, CCTV images of visibly covered women being attacked on London streets, pushed onto train tracks. Closer to home, graffiti appeared on the building where she lived. "*Go home*" was scrawled in black paint on the exterior walls.

Down below the pavement of thick snow, under the tombstone grey of the Tube station, she carried Inara down the steps. Newspapers flew about, scattering the news like haunting shadows fluttering around her. Waiting at the platform, she looked around at a group of young men laughing and joking with each other. They stopped when she looked at them. She turned back around quickly, staring down onto the drop below to the rails of the train tracks. She held Inara close, feeling her frail body like a small bag of flour in her arms. The group of men sniggered in the distance. She was sure they were walking towards where she and Inara stood, close to the tracks. She stepped back slowly, trying to distance herself from the gap. She closed her eyes as the train whizzed past her, as she felt her heart beating against Inara's body. The train ground to a halt and the red trimmed doors opened, exhaling as she did when she walked on. She sat hiding her bundle underneath her clothes, protecting her from the cold, watching as people exchanged glances, some hopping off the train, just before the doors closed. She sat there alone, wondering how things had changed. How at first, she hadn't noticed the signs that she stood out. Maybe they hadn't been there. Maybe the world around her was shifting instead.

She looked at her reflection in the window and pushed her scarf back. She was beginning to understand what Laila had said back at the community centre. She left it on, unable to take off the only link that reminded her of who she was. She pushed Inara off the Tube and tried to shake off the stares and suspicions, unsure if they were real or if she had become increasingly nervous since Nidal – if his death was because someone wanted revenge for what they had exposed or if it was because they were Muslim. Since she also couldn't trust her own mind, she had a difficult time translating situations and potential threats, real or imagined. Her counsellor had told her it might happen; that she would suffer from anxiety and heart palpitations.

The days rolled into each other. Since Inara was born, Reem couldn't return to her hotel work. She awoke early and sometimes waited all day for dawn to break, but the sun shone meekly and barely broke through the cloud cover. Reem hadn't ever known the sun to be so dull. It was a cold Reem had never felt before. It crept into the thin walls of the apartment and she was worried that Inara would feel it through the layers of the blankets she had wrapped her in.

Leah had stayed with her since she had discovered her father's involvement in the building. She refused to be associated with who they had become. Reem felt that she needed to be around her and to be closer to Mo, although they both barely saw anyone. They simply went through the motions of the days.

The flat was even smaller than the last one. It had two bedrooms and a tiny kitchen area that consisted of a basic fridge, cooker, sink and some worktop. The lounge had two old sofas and the windows were only dressed because Laila had given her some old curtains of hers. The monotonous days, staring at the same old walls, and the view of the blackened tower out of her window were not helping their recovery. Reem missed her English classes and even missed working at the hotel. She missed seeing Kesandu and Archie and hearing their stories about their home countries. There was something about sharing them that made the spaces they inhabited, the world they shared, seem less claustrophobic and dreary. She had avoided seeing anyone she loved. Anxious that her involvement with them would bring about their ruin, as it had done with Nidal.

They were both shocked to hear a knock at the door. Neither of them was expecting anybody.

'Who is it?' Reem shouted through the door.

'It's me, Jane.'

The two women looked around the apartment. It was a mess – the baby wasn't changed and there were dirty dishes in the sink and bedding on the sofa. They scrambled round as fast as they could, but Jane kept knocking.

'Please open the door or I will have to report that you refused entry.'

'No, no, we are coming.' Reem ran over and opened the door, flustered. 'Jane, we didn't know you were coming.'

'I just came to see how you both are. Leah, how are you?'

'Don't pretend you're bothered now I don't have a child for you to take,' Leah scoffed.

'Leah!' Reem said, shocked that Leah had said it out loud.

'I'm sorry you feel like that, Leah. I know this is a difficult time for you,' Jane said, turning to Reem, 'for the whole community. How are you, Reem?'

'I am fine. Thank you.' Her response was stiff.

'Is there anything you need help with?'

'No.'

'Reem, I am concerned that you aren't coping. Temporary care for Inara can be arranged.'

'You mean take her away?'

'She will still be your child, Reem, but it might give you the time you need to get sorted.'

'No, you can't take her. I won't let you.' Reem ran over to Inara and grabbed her, holding her closely but disturbing her in the meantime, causing her to wail.

'It won't be up to you.' Jane paused. 'Or me. The courts will decide.'

Reem tried desperately to quieten Inara down but her heightened state of emotions just seemed to make everything worse. 'You can't. She's my baby.'

Leah walked over and took Inara off her, pointing at the sofa, encouraging Reem to sit down.

'What if we do it together?' Leah said, lulling Inara back to a more peaceful state. 'You know how hard it's been. Don't make it worse for us,' Leah said to Jane, as she placed

Inara calmly into her cot. She turned to Reem. 'I'll help you, Reem. I will stay here. We'll get work between us, clean the place up. We won't lose another child.'

Reem was in shock. She couldn't speak. She didn't understand how a stranger could take someone else's baby. How government care could be better than a mother's care. She thanked God that Leah was there, her voice smoothing things over, understanding the complicated legal words Jane was using. Reem blocked out everything and watched Inara now playing innocently in her cot. Inara was all Reem had left. She couldn't lose her.

Chapter 19

~ Leah ~

The tower remained, unwavering against the dull sky. When the snow fell on the glassless window frames of the tower, it heaped up so at night it looked like the disturbed soil of freshly dug graves. Sometimes Leah woke up hearing the screams from it. She lived with it in her shadow, always there, reminding her. Slowly, the open wound became less tender, but she felt how she imagined an amputee must. That something was missing. Sometimes she woke up and felt him there next to her. But once she opened her eyes fully and escaped her dreams, she remembered he wasn't.

Leah couldn't bear to be back in the hospital. She wasn't ready to be in the same place Elijah was last. It brought back too many painful memories. Her parents didn't know where she was, and Leah preferred it that way. It was too much to know of their involvement and all she could do was take one day at a time.

Leah stayed with Reem and together they passed the days slowly. Leah had Inara when Reem went looking for jobs and sat with her through the evenings when Reem secured work, washing up at a restaurant twenty minutes away.

When it was Leah's turn to be with Inara, it reminded her of the times she had spent with Elijah when he was that age. It was a beautiful time and she remembered how her days were spent feeding him, rocking him to sleep and seeing how content he was. She bent down to kiss Inara's soft cheeks. Elijah would have loved to meet her, Leah thought.

'I wonder if you will like treasure hunting or digging for dinosaur bones?' Leah cooed. She didn't imagine it would, but looking at Inara's face light up and smile whenever she spoke to her made Leah feel better. Holding her and being close to her, feeling her warmth, seeing her tiny lips move, her eyes staring into hers, she couldn't help but care about her and feel needed whenever she cried and stuck out her tiny arms, wanting to be carried. Leah even found herself missing her at work and looking forward to going home to her.

They both kept the place clean and bought food together. Reem taught Leah how to cook Syrian food. At the weekends, Reem showed her how to make the traditional mezze breakfasts that Reem once enjoyed with her family. There were a dozen dishes. Thick, creamy yoghurt sprinkled with mint and drizzled with olive oil. She would mash fava beans and dress them with garlic chilli and olive oil and add chopped tomatoes on top. Other plates of fried egg cooked with garlic and tomatoes, mint tea and bulgur wheat. During the evenings Reem had off, she would show her the meals she could make and it reminded Leah of when she had last cooked with Elijah. How he would have filled a space there with them. But she felt that he hadn't truly left her. He was just waiting.

Leah loved those cooking days the most because she imagined she was somewhere else. Reem did too. There was a simplicity in preparing good food that transported them all to a warm landscape, a country far away from the ice-cold winter and bleak nights. The jewelled pomegranate seeds topped off the mezze and salads. The lamb was slowly cooked and fell apart in the rice, served with cool yoghurt. Reem would tell Leah about her favourite foods and when it was prepared, at celebrations like Eid and people's weddings. The memory of happy times and the future of making some of their own were almost in reach. Reem told stories to Inara and Leah listened as the warmth from the rising ochre sun penetrated the cheerless, cold room. She listened as the vibrant, ancient streets came to life in the space between them. Leah wanted to immerse herself in it just as Elijah had done and now, she was beginning to understand why he had loved it so much.

As life became easier for the both of them, the days flew by. Jane visited almost every week and was pleased with the progress they had made. Inara was no longer required to have a social worker. It was with this unexpected celebratory feeling that resembled some goodness that she decided it was a perfect time to do something else she had been putting off.

'I am going to speak to Mo.'

'Are you sure that's a good idea?' Reem said, feeding Inara some egg.

'I need to do this,' Leah said, standing up and taking a deep breath.

Reem didn't say anything else.

Mo had secured a flat in the same vicinity but in a different building. She followed his footsteps across the grass, where he had left her standing before. She walked over to the building, her hands sweating slightly despite the cold air. Her fingers quivered over the lift button, just long enough to almost make her change her mind, but she stayed strong and pressed it firmly. She took a deep breath before knocking on the door. Leah knew that he wouldn't want to invite her in, but she didn't want to do this in the hallway.

'Please, Mo, it won't take a minute.'

He opened the door so she could step inside. She looked out of the window, preferring to keep her back to him as she began.

'Leah, if it's about Elijah...'

Hearing his name threw her off focus. 'No, it isn't. It's about me.'

Mo sat down, ready to listen. Leah looked at his arm, still in a sling, and the new scarring on his face. She wanted to ask him how he was, how he was coping after Nidal, but she knew that if she stalled for too long, she would lose the courage to say what she had come for.

'Mo. I have thought about this before, and now, well, it just all makes sense to me.' Leah paused, hoping for Mo to say something, anything. He didn't, so she turned around. 'I want you, Mo. You're the one who was there for me. You're the only one I see who doesn't need anyone else.'

'Look, Leah, I don't need anyone not because I'm special –'

'But you are, Mo. I see it in ways I don't see in anyone else.'

'Leah, listen. What I have, what you want. You don't need me for it.'

'I don't understand –'

'You say I don't need anyone but that's because I have guidance through my faith. Every quality you see that's good in me is because of my faith.'

'Yes, and I am ready for that too. I want to be that person. I can be. I've learnt about it. Reem has been explaining it to me and I love everything I know about your religion.'

'This is your journey, Leah. You don't need me...'

'Mo, please. I know you can be the one. We can get married, I respect that is what you need. I want to have a part of your strength, your faith –'

'And you can. But you need to find yourself first.' Mo disappeared and brought out a box of tissues. Leah didn't even realise she was crying. 'When was the last time you felt you were doing what your soul wanted? Follow it, Leah. Allah will not let you down.'

'But there is no one else I want.'

'I am not what you want. Every strength of mine you want is from my faith. You can have that without having me.'

Leah didn't know what else to say. She was so sure that she had it figured out, that he was the key. She walked out onto the landing and down the staircase. An empty part of her was reopening inside her, like all the healing she had been through had amounted to nothing. The wound was opening and even the thought of Inara, of Reem, wasn't enough to fill it. She looked at Reem's building and it was too close to Mo's. It was too close to the tower. She knew what she had to do. Without thinking, she headed straight to the hospital, threw the card away from Jonathan, bypassed the wards and headed to the charity department.

'Doctors without Borders,' she said to the admin staff at the desk. 'Sign me up. I want to go as soon as possible.'

'I recognise you,' the clerk said, peering over the desk.

'Yes, I used to work here.'

'No, not from here... you were the first doctor on the scene at the north London mosque attack. I remember now.'

Leah carried on writing, unwilling to look up and show her flushed cheeks.

'The doctor on duty that night said that if you hadn't been there, we would have lost two more.'

Leah could feel her heart thudding loudly in her ears. She must have meant Mo and Ali. She began to cry silently and the clerk passed her some tissues.

'You were close to them?'

Leah nodded. 'Yes, I was. I am.'

Leah handed the form back and the few minutes the clerk took to look over it was just long enough for her to take in some deep breaths and blot her eyes.

'Do you have a particular region you're interested in?'

Leah said it almost without thinking. 'The Middle East.'

As soon as she had said it, a ripple of nerves fluttered through her body. It was the right choice for her and she didn't doubt it for a second. She wanted to be a part of Reem's world, the beauty of what she and Mo found in it. The love of it had seeped through into her being and she wanted to explore it for herself.

***

On the way back home, she visited her old neighbourhood. She passed her old house. She went up to the front door and knocked. No one answered. She peered around to the side of the house and saw that the back gate was left slightly ajar. She walked down the path and pushed it, opening it out into the garden. The grass had grown long and weeds had overtaken the once manicured flowered beds. The swing in the trees was broken and hung down, tangled in the long, cold grass. The roses had died. Snapped off in the depths of the winter cold. As she walked through the garden, she spotted the beehive at the end. It was silent. She opened it up and looked inside. There were no bees. Just rotting wood, an empty hive, and shredded pieces of what was once golden honeycomb.

chapter 20

~ Reem ~

Since Leah had left she hadn't seen many people, and she felt it was time to go and get out into the world more. Mahmoud had called her every few days to check on her and when he said he had important news, Reem arranged to go and meet him at Edgware Road for some lunch.

Mahmoud was waiting for her at the Syrian restaurant that Reem had had dinner at all those months ago. From the outside, the restaurant looked less inviting. The puddles of water on the pavement had been splashed up the sides of the windows, smearing them with speckles of mud. The Arabic sign was half scratched off and faded. Reem picked up the menu and realised she was now reading the English fluently. She had spent a lot of time at home watching the news, documentaries and films with Arabic subtitles and she had a little waver of hope that things were picking up.

Reem sat down. Inara had fallen asleep in her push-chair and Mahmoud was busy telling the waiter his order. She liked it when he spoke in Arabic. It reminded her of the same boy she knew. When he spoke in English, he changed. He seemed less confident, more uncertain of what he was saying. It was a side of him she hadn't seen before.

Reem watched as the waiters brought out food to neighbouring tables that were beginning to fill up for lunch time. She closed her eyes and imagined she was miles away in her favourite restaurant in Syria, which sat on a hilltop overlooking the city. The aromas made her hungry. She often forgot to eat these days. Sometimes it became easier not to eat and cheaper, so she could pay the rising heating bills to keep the flat warm enough for Inara in the winter. It had turned into a habit. She still felt like the nourishment of food was a pleasure she didn't deserve.

But when the food was brought out – the cooked fish, the grapevine leaves stuffed with mince, the lamb stew – she ate and began to feel better. Mahmoud gave her spoonfuls of the spicy soup then ladled the sauce onto her rice, sprinkling it with extra currants – because she used to steal his as a child, he reminded her – and she ate until she felt full. She only became nervous right at the end, at the thought of paying the bill. She picked up the menu and scanned the prices, trying to work out how much it would cost, how much it would set her back in her tight budget for the month.

'Are you still hungry?' Mahmoud said, watching her reading the menu.

'No, no,' Reem said, putting it down.

'I invited you, Reem, don't worry about it.'

Reem leant over the table and whispered to him, 'You can't afford this.'

'There's a reason I invited you here today. I have some good news.'

Reem sat back and for some reason, she felt worried. Like she had avoided him all this time and now he was probably going to leave her. The thought of not seeing him, of not having him around, became painful.

'What is it?'

'Don't look so worried,' he laughed. 'You are now looking at the proud owner of the Noor Furniture company!'

'What?' said Reem. As it sunk in, she carried on, 'You own the business now?'

'No, no. But I have been saving since I worked there and now I have bought my own tools and I have a workshop – not very big, but big enough. And I just got my business cards printed,' Mahmoud said, pulling a stack of freshly printed cards and handing one to Reem. 'And I already have my first order.'

'*Alhamdulilah* that's brilliant news, Mahmoud! *Mabrook*.'

Mahmoud beamed as he told Reem about how he had been working for clients for years and when they heard he was leaving, the furniture they wanted became more affordable. Since he didn't have the overheads like his employer did, he could sell them for a cheaper price, so he began the business with orders already streaming through the door.

'I have orders for large pieces of furniture too, and my dad's old friend in Syria is arranging the mother of pearl to be imported so I can get back to the traditional way of working. But this time, for myself and a few other migrants that I have met along the way. I can give them better hours, working conditions and pay.'

'That really is such good news. But I thought that you would never do what your dad did? That's what you used to say.'

'I was a kid back then, Reem. We all have dreams, but it isn't about dreaming. It is about making the most of what we have. What we have now, what we can have in our future, and changing with the times as you grow. It may be that we thought something was bad for us, but in fact it is good.'

Reem thought about that. The last line she was sure was a verse from the Qur'an. "*And it may be that you dislike a thing which is good for you.*" She wondered about herself. She had been given a new life. It had stemmed from pain and trauma but she was alive today. She was eating and breathing and she had her baby next to her. She scooped up Inara in her hands and held her close. Inara opened her eyes and began to cry.

'Ah, she is hungry. She has smelt home and now will only eat this,' Mahmoud said, laughing.

Reem smiled and fed her some rice and soup.

'There's something else.' Mahmoud's tone changed. It was more serious. 'I have something for both of you.'

'What is it?'

Reem looked at the table. Sat in the centre of it was a crushed blue velvet box. She didn't move. She kept her hands tucked under the table.

'Well, aren't you going to look inside?'

Reem hesitated, then cracked open the box. Inside was a ring. A trio of stones made of lapis lazuli, inset into twenty-four carat gold.

Reem gasped, unable to believe what she was looking at. She took it out of the box and turned it over. He couldn't have found one almost identical to the one she had been searching for. She twisted it until she could see the inside of the gold band. The Arabic inscription was there: "*And He has put love and mercy between your hearts.*"

She began to cry. 'Where did you get this? It looks just like my mother's.'

'It is. She gave it to me. Years ago, when we were still in school.'

'I thought it had been sold. I've been looking for it. Even over here, I saw Syrian antiques in the shop next door and went in to look. I couldn't go past a jewellery shop without checking. I must have searched half of Syria.'

'I'm sorry, Reem. I had no idea. I thought about giving it to you so many times, but it was never the right time and so I kept it with me just in case. You deserve more than what I could have offered you, but now with the business, and well –'

'You said a gift for both of us?'

'Yes, I want to take care of you. Both of you,' he said, kissing Inara on the forehead. 'If you will have me.'

***

Leah wrote regularly and Reem always saved her post-cards and letters. She reread them often when she missed her and read them to Inara, showing her the photographs that she sent along too. Leah looked happy.

Dear Reem,

My first posting is in Gaza. I'm staying in an old ho-tel near the coast here and I'm awoken most nights by the sound of gunfire or rockets in the air. One fell close to the hotel a few nights ago, and the loud scream of it hasn't left my eardrums.

Every day I treat victims of war and I think of you. How strong you must be to be as you are. Always keep that innocence, Reem. The world is better for it.

The days are keeping me busy and there are so many people to see. London seems calm compared to here.

I feel guilty when I can show my passport and leave. I have privileges I hadn't ever considered. Speaking of leav-

ing, I am going to cover the West Bank in a few days, in Palestinian occupied territories. I hope I get the chance to visit Jericho there. It's one of the earth's oldest cities. How Elijah would have loved to have seen it! I thought I would feel further apart from him out here, but in an odd way, he feels closer.

How is Inara? I miss her. Send me some photos in your next letter.

Your friend,
Leah

Dear Reem,

I made it to Jericho in the West Bank in Palestine. It is a beautiful old city. It reminds me of the stories you used to tell and I wonder if it is similar to Syria in some ways, like the landscape? Jericho sits in a wadi, surrounded by mountains. It's filled with religious tourists and old stories that come alive on its streets.

The archaeological site sits beneath the mountain. It's one of the oldest city remnants in the world. There is something about being here that makes me feel better. I don't know what it is, but despite the work, the injustice, I feel a sort of peace here that I never did before. Maybe it's the distance or the simple way of life, but one I feel I have been missing out on.

Your friend,
Leah

Dear Reem,

I've been in Jordan for the last couple of months and I completed my training at a hospital there. I meet so many people through my work. Today I met three sisters who were refugees from Syria. They told me about their ex-

pectations for school, but when they were forced to flee, they couldn't afford to go to school anymore so they pick potatoes for a couple of dollars a day. There are so many refugee camps here and so many refugees that I think my work will never be complete.

I thought I would always be too hurt to care for children, but something's changed. I feel better when I'm working with them. I love their hope. It makes me feel hopeful despite the world falling apart around us. I hear it through countless stories of people helping each other. Of families sharing their last meal, of parents who go hungry for their children. People who live for a higher purpose. It is this hope I want to hold on to and never let go. So I've decided to specialise to become a paediatrician.

Your friend,
Leah

***

Reem missed Leah at the wedding but she sent her photographs and a short letter saying that they were doing fine, and that they had moved into another apartment close to Mahmoud's workshop. It was a ground floor apartment on a busy high street, but it was set back enough so that the noise didn't filter through. It even had a small patch of grass out the back as their garden, which Reem relished.

As soon as Reem moved in she planted their own pomegranate tree in the soil against the back wall, so each day when she was washing up, or hanging the clothes outside, or watching Inara play, she could see the tree. She knew that it would take time to heal, and the tree reminded her of that. It reminded her of the pomegranate trees back home in her family's courtyard. How her mother had told her it grew in the gardens of paradise. This piece of her homeland, anchored in her garden, transporting her. It also connected Adar and Elijah, and yet belonged to neither of them. It grew slowly, sprouting at first and then getting stronger as each day passed. When the wind was bad, she would move it inside and when the weather was cold, she would wrap it in a plastic bag to keep the frost out. When a branch snapped, she would plant another seed and slowly one took hold of the soil in the back and found its roots in the earth. And when it was time, its solid scarred skin would produce hidden jewels in its centre.

As Inara grew, she played outside more and helped Reem to care for the pomegranate tree. Reem could almost see the future, one where they could make their own memories, their own life for Inara, and although that would be different to the one they experienced, she could tell her stories of their homeland. Reem began to write them down. Mahmoud carved them into Inara's furniture. Reem cooked them in the house. A house where now their stomachs were full each day, where the sound of fireworks no longer had them ducking for cover. Inara could enjoy things that they never had as a child and although the city was changing around them, she still saw hope and goodness in the people she met.

Reem visited David, who she had met at the British Museum, and was offered a job as assistant curator for the Middle East exhibition. Behind the scenes at the museum, Reem saw the number of collectibles that passed through the doors. Some were donated, others were bought and sold. The antique shops around London began to fill with remnants of families' histories. Their heirlooms and their inheritances, sold for cash to survive.

On her way out she saw the lives of those who had passed on, who had lost things that were now showcased in glass cabinets, in glass jars. It gave her an uneasy feeling. It reminded her of the preservation of the dead back in the Natural History Museum. It reminded her of the organs trafficked and sold on the black market.

Antiquities were displayed in people's homes, behind glass doors, showcasing a stolen piece of history; one that perhaps didn't exist anymore, except in parts around the world. Scattered. Displaced. The parts of us that make us whole. It wasn't long after this, that Reem left the museum. She had always dreamed of being in that role, working with historical relics, piecing together the past. But Syria's landscape had changed so dramatically that it would never be like it was. There was too much that had happened for it to ever be the land it once was to her. But now her experiences meant that she no longer valued land as much as she used to. Instead, she became more interested in life.

Dear Reem,

I am sorry it's been such a long time since I wrote to you last. Thank you for the photographs of Inara. She is so beautiful. She looks just like her mum. I read that her name means 'illuminating'. Yes, I am learning Arabic, in'shaa'Allah (excuse my handwriting)!

I am so sad I missed your wedding, but it gives me comfort to see how beautiful the day was and I'm happy knowing you have found each other. To know you and Inara are taken care of gives me so much peace of mind.

The evenings here are warm and I can hear the sound of cicadas in the grass, and smell the heady scent of jasmine flowers as I sit in my hotel writing to you. I am back in Palestine and have been placed near Jerusalem. I'm vis-

iting for the weekend and from almost every angle, I can see the gleam of gold in the Dome of the Rock.

It is beautiful. It reminds me of when you told me you used to pray towards Al-Aqsa mosque. I am so close, I couldn't resist going to see it. It sits in a wide, spacious courtyard in the centre of a souk that winds like a labyrinth through the old city. I can see why you miss the souks. I get lost in them for hours.

In the centre is the gold-topped Dome of the Rock. Down the steps past it is an area I thought was a fountain, but when I looked closely at the stone seats and the taps that sprout from the stone, I realised it is where you wash for the prayers.

I stood in front of Al-Aqsa mosque and it is beautiful. Inside it has deep red carpets, with trims of golden shapes. Above the centre of the mosque, a huge crystal chandelier hangs from the ceiling and it's decorated in the most beautiful geometric patterns throughout. I wish one day that you could see it.

I couldn't spend long there as I am heading to Ramallah, the main city in the West Bank, and I imagine I will be based there for a few months. I miss you both. But sometimes at night, I gaze at the stars and I know that in one way or another, we all see the light from them. It gives me comfort to know that.

Send my love to your illuminating star.

Your friend,

Leah

***

Reem didn't see the wedding coming. According to Laila, it was a shock to her too. 'My five-year term as an asylum seeker is up next year, and I was wondering how I would find a way to stay if the government doesn't grant me refugee status.'

'*Alhamdulilah*, that's great news, Laila,' Reem said and hugged her. 'Why didn't you tell me you were worried about it?'

'There was nothing you could do – or me, even! So I didn't want to burden you. You already have enough on.'

'When is the wedding?'

'Next week. Actually, I was wondering if you wouldn't mind doing me a favour?'

'*In'shaa'Allah*, name it.'

'Do you want to throw my henna party?' Laila looked shy, as though there was no one else to ask, or as though she didn't think she even deserved one.

'I would love to! So, who is the man who saved you?' Reem asked, fluttering her eyes.

'I believe you two have already met,' Laila said in the same joyful tone, as Mo left the men's section of the mosque.

Reem gasped. 'Mo?'

Laila nodded and flashed an antique gold ring, inset with rubies on her right hand.

The wedding was an intimate ceremony, taking place a few weeks later in the local registry office. It was a room that seated fifty people, but only about twenty attended. The couple wanted to keep it low-key. Chairs remained empty, reminding them of their missing loved ones. Reem sat in the chairs as they said their vows. She looked through the steamed up windows as she left, back into the hall inside. The lights glittered from the chandeliers as two people began a new life, out of the ashes of the ones they left behind.

***

Two years passed. They were entering their second summer since the fire and the plants and greenery had started to climb up the tower, turning it into a living part of the grounds.

Ramadan came around again and a leaflet for a Big Iftar was posted through Reem's door. The evening was still light with dusk only just breaking. There on the grass, the long stretch of rugs were laid out, lamps hung from trellis, and wires hung between two poles that stretched across the grass. She saw Mo and Laila. Mahmoud was with them. Brianna had made it, and many others she spotted from the community centre. Mo's voice rang out the call to prayer and they stood in line, praying on the fresh green grass, the sound of their children playing around their feet. This year the rows were longer. There was more than double the amount of people than the year before. Kesandu was there too. Despite the large crowd, Reem felt Leah's absence acutely. She missed how they used to laugh together and how she reminded her of Elijah. Reem couldn't help but catch glimpses of him amongst the children, but when they turned around, it was never him. Her eyes began to well with tears and made her vision blurry. She saw the crowd as one, and she was on the edge, looking over them all in the distance. Between the buildings, groups of people were walking over to see what was happening and amongst them, a solitary figure walked. It was a familiar walk she had seen before. Reem walked towards it, rubbing her eyes to see more clearly. It couldn't be. She barely recognised the woman standing in front of her. She was dressed in light linens, her hair lighter, braided to one side and without a scrap of make up on her now tanned cheeks.

'Leah, is that you?' Reem said, as Leah twirled around.

'I thought I would surprise you!' Leah said, wrapping her arms around her.

Reem was speechless.

'Look at you, and Inara!' Leah said, scooping her up in her arms.

'What a blessing you made it. I can't believe you're here. How come? When did you come back?'

'Don't worry, we have plenty of time to catch up. I'm here for a while. It's just so good to see you both. I missed you so much.'

'We did too!'

Their reunion was interrupted by Mo, who had walked over with Laila.

'Laila, I want to introduce you to a good friend of ours. This is Leah.' Mo gestured towards Leah and she leaned forward to kiss Laila on the cheeks. 'This is my wife and our little one, Nidal.'

Leah almost cried. It was a perfect name and he shared his uncle's deep, hazel coloured eyes. Leah watched as Laila ran off after him, as he crawled towards the food, over crockery, used plates and people.

'I'm sorry about what happened before, Mo. You know, before I left,' Leah said, looking down as she spoke to him.

'There's nothing to apologise for. That was years ago. And you saved my life.'

'You saved mine, in a way I hadn't thought possible. And you were right. About everything.'

'*Alhamdulilah*,' Mo said, kicking the floor with his feet like Nidal used to. 'You're happy?'

Leah looked up to the stars. '*Alhamdulilah*, I'm getting there.'

Reem watched them both and the gathering of everyone out underneath the night sky. She looked at Leah, Mo, Laila, Brianna, Kesandu, and the community who had come out to support one another. The people she'd known from home, from her journey here. Those that helped in the aftermath of the fire. The people who had lost loved ones and were still determined make other people's lives better, through life-changing acts of bravery and selflessness, to the smallest good deed. All of it made a difference to people's lives.

The full moon shone behind the silhouette of the tower, lighting up the windows as though the residents were home. The emptiness of it, the loss, created an ache in her heart. But when she felt herself about to give up hope, she was reminded in the light of the moon and in the vastness of the sky. She was reminded that there was more that lay beyond the earth and its war-torn lands. There was an existence above the ashes of what was left behind, in a world robbed of its riches and of its people. Reem remembered the promise of the sun rising from the West, signalling that there will be no more to take from the earth. How the earth will throw up everything buried beneath it. Then, the stars will disappear from an oil-red sky. The moon will split in half. The seas will rage in flames of fire. Everything will come to an end except for what goodness your hands sowed forth. Reem glanced upwards and realised the sky reflected the earth; darkness sprinkled with light. The most anyone can do is illuminate, and that was the role she had set for herself. She would fight to create light amidst the darkness.

CPSIA information can be obtained
at www.ICGtesting.com
Printed in the USA
BVHW080826080519
547715BV00003B/220/P